A LITTLE BIT
Sinful

A FORBIDDEN LOVE NOVEL

A LITTLE BIT
Sinful

A FORBIDDEN LOVE NOVEL

ROBYN DEHART

Entangled Publishing, LLC
2614 South Timberline Road
Suite 109
Fort Collins, CO 80525
Visit our website at www.entangledpublishing.com.

Scandalous is an imprint of Entangled Publishing, LLC.

Edited by Alethea Spiridon Hopson
Cover Design by Heidi Stryker

ISBN 978-1-943892-40-2

Manufactured in the United States of America

First Edition March 2013

Scandalous
an Entangled imprint

To my brother, Rick, for taking his lovely bride-to-be to the bookstore on their 3rd date to show her his "famous romance novelist" sister's books. And to Barbara, welcome to the family. I'm so glad y'all finally found your happily ever after.

And as always to my husband, Paul...as the saying goes, "sometimes in the middle of an ordinary life, love gives us a fairy tale," you're definitely mine.

Prologue

LONDON, OCTOBER 1875

Clarissa Kincaid wanted to scream, wanted to the run through the house pulling at her hair. Instead, she settled for a calmer, though nonetheless equally unladylike, groan.

Her aunt sat with a letter from her sister in Cornwall. She didn't bother looking up. "What is it this time?" Aunt Maureen asked from the settee.

"Another denial letter from Mr. Franklin." Clarissa slammed the letter down on the desk and blew out a breath. "I have lost my patience with that man."

"Oh dear." Maureen dropped the letter, then wrapped her handkerchief around her fingers again and again. "What are we to do if the man refuses to deal with us? We shall certainly starve if he will not release monies to us."

Clarissa resisted the urge to roll her eyes. Aunt Maureen had always been somewhat on the dramatic side. "We are not going to starve. Settle yourself, Aunt Maureen. I shall think of something." Her eldest brother, the earl, had been dead a little over two months now and they had survived on the remainder of Aunt Maureen's savings, which hadn't been much. But they were running out. Clarissa still had some money hidden away, but she was saving it until they absolutely had to use it. She had been attempting to work with their family solicitor, but he "refused to entertain requests from any woman." The narrow-minded fool insisted on hearing directly from the new earl, Clarissa's other brother, Marcus. The only problem with that was that Marcus had been gone for nearly ten years and no one had any idea when he'd return. Or if he'd return.

"Well, this is simply unacceptable, Clarissa, there must be something we can do," Maureen said. Her handkerchief now sat in a sad little ball upon her lap and she'd begun working the fabric of her skirt.

Clarissa needed to think of something soon before her aunt had worn through all of her clothing.

"If only we had a more reasonable solicitor to work with," Maureen said. "Someone who would allow us some say in the matter, or at the very least be willing to communicate with us. This is…this is simply dreadful."

"Precisely." Maureen was right. They needed a different solicitor, but where would they find one willing to work with them? And how was she to dismiss Mr. Franklin if he refused to communicate with her? Then it hit her, the idea forming in her mind rapidly. She pulled out a piece of parchment from her late brother's desk and poised pen over the paper. "You are brilliant!"

"I am. I am?" She eyed Clarissa suspiciously. "I know that look, dear. What are you doing?"

"Something I should have done shortly after Charles died. I am dismissing our current solicitor and hiring a new one."

Aunt Maureen shook her head in confusion. "Need I remind you that you do not have the authority to do such a thing?"

"It is not I," Clarissa said in her most innocent voice. "This letter shall come from Marcus. It is time for him to do something worthwhile for this family."

"And you know of a solicitor who will work with us until Marcus returns home?" Maureen asked.

"Not exactly." Clarissa smiled. "But I hear that Mr. Ignatius F. Bembridge, LLB is quite forward in his thinking."

Maureen frowned. "Who might he be, dear?"

Clarissa stood, leaned forward across the desk holding out her hand toward her aunt. "Mr. Ignatius F. Bembridge at your service. A pleasure to meet you."

"Oh, we are doomed," Maureen said, not bothering to shake Clarissa's hand.

Clarissa stepped around the desk and went and sat next to her aunt. "Do not fret. I shall study Charles' books and learn about our properties and what needs to be done. But someone needs to be in charge of things until Marcus can return. It might as well be me." Clarissa shrugged. "It will at the very least give us access to the funds right now. And I shall write another letter to Thomas Adventure Tours. Perhaps they can find my wayward brother."

"Good heavens, child, what if someone discovers what you're about?" She retrieved her sad wad of a handkerchief and began to worry the fabric again.

"They won't. It shall be our little secret."

Chapter One

Clarissa was in love.

As fortune would have it, she was fairly certain that he felt the same for her. She smiled up at George Wilbanks as he walked next to her in the park. He was so handsome with his dark blond hair and striking green eyes. Every woman in London envied her time with George, but it had become quite evident that he only had eyes for her. He never took any other girls to the park for a walk.

He always brought her daisies, which had never been her favorites, but she knew that they meant love. Though there were some who would argue they meant innocence, but what did they know? It had also been a full two months since he danced more than one dance a night with any girl other than her. But in Clarissa's mind, the walk was proof enough.

This had become a ritual for them. Every Wednesday

afternoon they met and walked in the park, side-by-side, together, with her Aunt Maureen walking behind them several paces. Some days her friend Ella and her brother, Victor, would walk with them, but today, they were alone.

"The weather has been quite unpleasant lately," George said.

"Indeed. All the dampness, it's so dreary, not at all the manner of weather one would prefer for the Season." They had so much in common, agreed upon so many things. They would make a perfect pair. Some day when they were finally able to marry. At the moment, George was waiting. His father was stern and not an all-together pleasant man, and he was stingy with George's rightful inheritance. So George was reluctant to marry until he had complete control of the funds and the household. No one could blame him for such a thing. A man wanted to be in control of his own household.

"George, how is the future looking? Are you hopeful?" She wanted to come right out and ask him when are you going to propose, when do I get to finally be your wife? Even if they couldn't marry until his father had passed on, they could be engaged, so that the world knew she belonged to George Wilbanks, and that someday she'd be Lady Wilbanks. Despite all of that, she needed to be patient and give him time. Certainly it was only a matter of time. He had so much to manage with his father.

"The future looks good. Though you know my father is still as healthy as they come," he said with a chuckle. "Perhaps some would think I'm a black heart for speaking of my father in such a way. Who else is waiting for their own parent to die simply so they can begin living their life as they see fit? I do hope you don't think ill of me."

"No, of course not," she said, giving him a warm smile. "I know the truth. You've been a very patient son. Anyone would agree."

He gave her a wink. "You are such a gem, Clarissa, a true friend. I enjoy our talks.

"And if I would like to be more than a friend?"

He took her hand and placed a whisper of a kiss against her glove. "Patience, my sweet. You must know that I am not in a good place right now. With my inheritance, the title, my father."

"George, none of that matters as long as we can be together." She felt certain she would help him weather anything. And his inheritance didn't matter to her.

He stopped walking and led her over to a bench near a sculpture. He paused while a group of ladies walked arm-in-arm passed them. One of the women looked back over her shoulder and gave George a secretive smile. It was on Clarissa's mind to ask him about it, but he appeared to have not even noticed the woman.

"I must be honest with you." He looked around to ensure they were out of earshot from anyone else. "I owe a lot of money to a particular establishment, and I am trying to take care of the situation without alerting my father. Nothing can be done about my future," he said delicately, "until that matter is resolved."

She looked up at him and grabbed his hands, then came to her senses and abruptly dropped them. "George, I had no idea you were in such trouble. I have money." She placed her hand against her chest. "I've been saving for years. All you need do is simply tell me how much you owe and I shall loan the sum to you." Not only did she have her own money, but since taking over the family finances, she had made some very profitable investments. She had, as it turned out, quite the knack for it. Of course she couldn't tell George that.

He smiled wistfully. "I would never ask you to do such a thing."

"It is no bother. Honestly, I am not doing anything with the money. It was put away for such an occasion." If this was the only thing standing between her and George finally marrying, then she was ready, eager even, to hand over the entire amount she'd saved, plus some. She could probably offer him some advice on sound investments too, but she didn't want him to think poorly of her for handling the family's monies whilst her brother was gone.

He held a hand up and shook his head. "No. I refuse to take money from you."

She was quiet a moment, considering the situation. Evidently money was keeping them apart, yet George was obviously too proud to allow her to help. Men were peculiar about such matters. She considered for a moment telling him her secret that she was quite schooled in financial matters, but once he knew that about her, their courtship would most certainly end. Being so unconventional was certainly nothing to celebrate. "At the very least, will you tell me to whom you owe money?"

Another group of people passed by. Clarissa smiled and waved to those she knew.

"You will think ill of me." He looked away from her. His intense gaze settled on the shrubbery across from their bench.

"Never!" She shook her head. "That is impossible. You must know that I hold you in the highest regard."

He nodded, then came to his feet. "Rodale's. I don't expect

you to know what that is. A lady such as yourself, so genteel and proper, would not be aware of such establishments." He met her gaze. "It is a gaming hell. I'm afraid I've gotten into a bit of trouble with some of my wagers. It's a wretched vice, certainly not one acceptable to a fine, upstanding lady."

Gambling. She knew that some men struggled with the vice, but she had not expected it of her George. Still, it changed nothing with her feelings for him. If she was to be his wife, she would assist him in any way she could.

She stood and gave his arm a squeeze. "Do not fret over such matters. Your admission has changed nothing about you, in my eyes."

They began walking again. She knew what needed to be done now. If her suspicion was correct, then Rodale's could belong to only one man, and she felt certain Justin Rodale would do her a favor.

• • •

Clarissa had selected her attire with great care. She knew that during this particular outing she could not draw attention to herself, so she'd donned one of her black mourning dresses and a hat large enough to cover most of her face. When she'd purchased the hat, it had come with too much plumage and she'd ripped out the feathers leaving it a simple black hat with cream-colored chiffon ribbons. Even as modest as the hat was, she worried she'd stand out too much. She fretted over the hat the entire carriage ride.

Nerves beat wildly inside her stomach. This was not something she would normally do, going to visit a gaming hell, but she had no other choice. There was even an ancient proverb suggesting such a thing, requiring desperate measures during desperate times. The carriage rolled to a stop. She sat still, hands folded in her lap. Men's voices filled the street that awaited her.

The driver opened the door to the carriage and she did her best to gather her wits. She swallowed, willing herself to be brave. This was something that had to be done, especially if she wanted to be married by the end of the Season. Considering she was rapidly approaching four and twenty, she most assuredly wanted to be married as soon as was possible. Using that very thought to bolster her courage, she stepped down from the hired hack, and straightened her pelisse.

"Wait here for me," she told the driver. "And I shall pay you extra."

Despite the late hour, the street bustled with activity. She tried to glance around without revealing too much of her own identity, but she would draw even more attention if she fell on the street in a heap of black wool. Two men walked up the street toward her, presumably heading directly to the establishment she too sought. Clarissa realized with alarming clarity that she knew one of the men, had just danced with him the night before at the Millerton's ball. She stepped out of their way and looked down at her shoes. Both men stepped into the gaming hell and the door closed behind them.

For a moment she considered climbing back into the hack and going straight home. As it was, Aunt Maureen thought Clarissa had gone to bed early with a sour stomach. But she could not allow fear to prevent her from helping George. If she didn't take care of this matter now, there was no telling how long it would take George to handle it. No, this was something that had to be done. She felt for the bag at her wrist with all of her money tucked inside. With a hearty breath, she took the steps leading to the unmarked red door.

She didn't even have to knock, the door simply opened as she lifted her hand. Noise and smoke poured out of the door. She couldn't see much, but spied a buxom woman sitting atop a man's lap while he examined his cards. A large beefy man stepped into the doorway, effectively blocking her view of anything save his barrel chest.

She tilted her head to see his face, though kept one gloved hand to her hat in case she needed to quickly cover herself. His thick eyebrows rose as he took in the sight of her. "A lady don't have business here," he said brusquely.

"I should like—" She cleared her throat behind her black lace glove. "That is, I need to speak to Mr. Rodale, if you do not mind."

"Mr. Rodale is otherwise engaged," the man said, brazenly mocking her speech.

"I have it on good authority that he is here most nights."

Three men came up behind her. "Are you lost, my lady?" one of them asked, then laughed heartily.

The man at the door moved her aside and admitted the three men before once again blocking the door.

She grabbed the bag at her wrist, hoping the reminder of why she was here would push her forward. "It is imperative that I speak with him." She tapped her foot in hopes of appearing more courageous than she actually felt. "Now."

The man eyed her for another minute before making a low growly noise. "Wait there." Then he slammed the door in her face.

She moved over to the far side of the stoop to allow any other patrons to enter the establishment without her being in the way or really being seen. After what felt like a quarter of an hour a man stepped out of the building, the beefy man stood behind him. "That's her, said she had to speak with you. It was imperative." Again the man mocked her speech.

It was not her fault she was well bred and educated.

"I'll handle matters from here, Clipps. You go back inside and keep an eye on things." He turned to face Clarissa. "I am Mr. Rodale. What is so important?"

His voice was different than she remembered, deeper, darker even, but still that hint of a French accent he'd tried so hard to rid himself of when he was a boy.

"I need to speak to you," she said dumbly. She mentally shook herself, then took a chance and glanced up at him. From this angle, the best she could do was get a look at his cravat, which was loosely tied at best. Where they stood now, with the light hanging next to the door, anyone walking by could see her. "Could we speak down here on the street, where it is more private?" She didn't bother waiting for him to answer, merely took the steps back down to the sidewalk.

"What is this about?" he asked, his voice sharp with irritation.

She looked up at him again, this time tilting her neck far enough to see his face. She could see bits of the boy she knew in the man before her, the same amber-colored eyes and olive skin, but she had not been expecting him to be so startlingly handsome. So tall and athletic and masculine, he was beyond dashing. She sucked in her breath at the same time his brows shot up.

"Chrissy? Is that you?" He grabbed her by the elbow and pulled her more into the shadows.

She closed her eyes against the wretched childhood nickname. "Please do not call me that," she hissed. "In fact do not say my name at all. I should not be here, but I needed to speak to you immediately."

He grinned. "Miss me after all these years?"

"I do not." Though, admittedly, that smile of his did make her wonder what he'd been doing the last several years. She shook her head. Now was not the time to reminisce. "I came to discuss a certain debt with you. Can I be assured of your discretion?"

"Clarissa, you are affecting the discretion of my establishment by being here. This is no place for a woman of your breeding to be seen." He glanced around them to ensure they were still alone. "What the devil are you doing here? You could have sent a post."

"I would like to pay the debts of Mr. George Wilbanks."

His warm caramel eyes narrowed. "What?"

"You heard me." She indicated the purse hanging from her wrist. "I brought the funds, now if you could please tell me precisely how much he owes, I will gladly pay the sum."

"Have you completely lost your senses?" Justin's jaw clenched.

How had she not noticed his handsomeness when she was a girl? He'd simply been her brother's friend and one whom she hadn't even deemed appropriate for Marcus to have.

Justin Rodale was a bastard, by birth, if not behavior. He'd been wretchedly surly and nothing more than a troublemaker. Not at all the sort of friend the son of an earl should have. It hadn't mattered to Clarissa that Justin had gone to all the same schools as Marcus. And he had teased her mercilessly and insisted on calling her that wretched name. *Chrissy.*

"First of all, I do not have a running summary in my mind of how much each patron owes me," he said. "I have far too many patrons for that. Secondly, I am not at liberty to discuss a man's debts with a woman who is not either his mother or his wife, and even then I probably would still refuse to disclose information." He paused a moment and eyed her. "Who is this man to you, Chrissy?"

"A friend," she said carefully. There was no need to tell Justin any more than he needed to know. "The fact of the matter is, is that George is far too proud a man to accept a loan from me so I thought to pay off his debts myself."

A crowd of men poured out from the establishment and onto the streets. They spoke loudly, cursing and laughing. Clarissa looked down to her boots until they had all passed. One stopped just shy of her and she held her breath, afraid someone had recognized her, but the man started walking again.

"Do you know George?" she asked.

Justin nodded, drawing attention to his hair that he kept far too long. The waves at the back brushed his collar. Scandalously long. Not at all like George's hair, which he kept well trimmed and manicured. "I know who he is," Justin said.

"And will you allow me to pay off his debts?"

"I will not."

She frowned, wrapped her arms over her chest. "And precisely why not?"

"Because he doesn't owe me any money."

• • •

TWO MONTHS LATER

They had been at the tea and card party for nearly an hour, and Clarissa was already poised to stick a hatpin in her eye. Granted the average age of the women in the room hovered somewhere near half of a century, still, normally, Clarissa found it rather easy, if not enjoyable speaking to people. Today, though, she was in no mood to be congenial.

She had only recently passed through a personal scandal and fortunately came out on the other side with her reputation mostly unscathed, all thanks to her new sister-in-law, Vivian. It seemed much longer than a mere eight weeks since Clarissa's long-lost brother had returned to London and then met and married Vivian amidst a slight scandal of their own. Now the newlyweds were honeymooning. So Clarissa, was once again, left to her own devices, a situation her aunt said always got Clarissa in trouble.

"Clarissa, dear, it's your turn," Lady Vesper said gently.

Clarissa looked up at the older woman who smiled warmly at her. They were playing whist and it was her turn. She glanced at her cards and selected one at random and tossed it down. It was unusual for her to be feeling so disjointed and rather unsocial. But her dear friend, Ella, had expressed concern when they'd first arrived. Concern for her family's financial situation, a situation Clarissa felt certain she could help with. Despite the fact that Clarissa told Ella nearly everything, she had never disclosed to her friend when she'd begun posing as Mr. Ignatius F. Bembridge.

Suffice it to say, Clarissa was thoroughly distracted.

Normally she was able to put her focus directly on the people with whom she was conversing, but today her thoughts were elsewhere. So instead of listening to Lady Vesper recount all the hilarity she witnessed the night before between her dog and her husband, all Clarissa wanted to do was pull Ella aside and procure additional details of the situation. If she were to offer her help, well, Mr. Bembridge's help, then she needed to know what she'd be up against.

It wasn't in her nature to be so unconventional, at least it shouldn't be. Her late sister-in-law, Rebecca, would be so disappointed. Rebecca had been married to Clarissa's eldest brother and had practically raised her. The woman had done her level best to teach Clarissa to be a perfect lady, something she still strived for. Still, she'd done what she'd done out of necessity and damned if she couldn't do it again to assist her dearest of friends.

"Clarissa, it's your turn," Ella said, nudging her with her elbow. "Again. Honestly, you haven't paid a lick of attention to this game."

Clarissa looked up and smiled. "My apologies. I'm afraid I'm a little scattered today."

"I'll say," Ella said. She dropped her own card onto the table. "What has your mind so consumed?"

"She's probably mooning over that fellow she fancies so much," Lady Vesper said.

Lady Vesper's cousin, Agatha smiled. "Oh are you betrothed to a handsome gentleman."

Ella shot Clarissa a look.

"Nothing so official," Clarissa said.

"Oh, my apologies," Agatha said.

"It's no bother, truly." The last thing Clarissa wanted was for any of these women to pity her. She'd had more than her fair share of such glances to last her a lifetime. She'd always been the girl whose mother had died in childbirth.

Clarissa smiled reassuringly. "I'm merely a feather-brain today, I'm afraid."

Lady Vesper went back to talking about her dog.

Ella frowned at her. "What are you thinking about?"

"You, goose. I am concerned about what you told me. I do wish we could discuss it more. I believe I could help," Clarissa said.

Ella smiled. "Precisely what I was hoping you'd say. I know you've spoken so highly of Mr. Bembridge. I was hoping you could set up a meeting between him and my father."

Clarissa looked down at her cards and tossed one onto the table. "Yes, I'll see what I can do. He is rather shy, though. Painfully so, I'm told."

"Haven't you met him?" Ella asked.

"Not precisely."

Ella frowned. "Then how did you go about finding him?"

"I saw an advertisement. Can't recall where though," she said. She hated lying to her friend, but the truth would be devastating to Clarissa's reputation.

"I'm not certain my father would hire a solicitor he hadn't even met," Ella said.

If Marcus were here and not on his honeymoon, then perhaps he could vouch for Mr. Bembridge enough to convince Ella's father. What was it about men that they felt they could only trust information if it came from another man? But what other man was there for her to trust with this secret?

Chapter Two

Justin stood at the large window overlooking the gaming hell floor. Rodale's was full tonight. The card tables were full, as were the dice tables. Over in the far left corner a group of men huddled, cheering and passing the wager book around. At that moment Clipps, Rodale's assistant manager, stepped into the office.

"What has them so riled up tonight?" Justin asked.

"It would seem that Wilbanks fellow's father has made a decree that he must marry before the viscount dies. So they're making wagers on which chit he'll choose."

George Wilbanks. The same man Clarissa Kincaid had offered to pay off the debts only two months before, debts that hadn't even existed. Justin needed to get a look at that wager book, see if Chrissy's name was on the list. He'd wait until the excitement died down and then go take a peek.

A half an hour later Justin made his way downstairs to check out the wager book. It was filled with all manners of wagers, from what sex Lord Fairfield's new child would be to whether or not Fiona Miller would ever agree to one of the many proposals she'd received. And then Justin came to the page regarding George Wilbanks's situation. There was a list of girls, seven of them, and by each name there were stakes and odds, numbers, and projections.

Clarissa's name was, in fact, on there and she and one other girl were leading in the group. The two most expected to garner marriage proposals from Wilbanks. Justin knew that the entitled made wagers on everything, and among their favorite involved who would marry whom. But he'd never really paid much attention to it. Seemed a silly pastime to him.

Then again, Clarissa Kincaid had never made it on anyone's list. Justin might not be able to do anything about the wagering, but he could see what he could do to ensure Clarissa didn't find herself married to the lying ass.

. . .

The following night Clarissa attended the new exhibit at the Royal Academy of Music Museum. Aunt Maureen had already found a bench to sit upon with a friend of hers so they could "chat instead of milling about in the crowds," as she'd put it. But Clarissa was eager to see the exhibit, especially the original manuscripts from Beethoven.

Despite the fact that she knew George would not be in attendance,—he had never been much for museums— she had donned her new pink gown. She couldn't help but wonder where he would go this evening and with whom. Sabrina Richmond had said she'd heard that George had gone riding with Maryann Fields. On more than one occasion. Clarissa knew he danced with other women, but he'd always told her it was to keep up appearances until the time came for him to become engaged. But Maryann Fields was very pretty, and the whole notion of George spending time with her made her uneasy.

As she began walking through the exhibit, she saw several people she knew, but they seemed more interested in gossip than the items up for viewing. She smiled and waved and spoke when necessary, but she kept moving forward. The first thing she came to was the violin collection. The glass case displayed violins across the years, the intricate wood carvings so ornate on some and others plain. She'd never tried to play any other instruments, preferring the piano above all else. But were she to try another, the violin would be the one.

"Good evening, Chrissy," Justin Rodale's voice came from behind her.

She looked into the reflection of the glass and saw his tall form behind her. She turned around to face him and had to swallow hard. He looked so very dashing wearing all black except for the bright white of his cravat at his throat. His unfashionably long hair had been pulled to the back and tied in a ribbon at his neck. It had been a couple of months since she'd seen him and he looked devastatingly handsome.

"You look like a pirate," she said dumbly. *Splendid*. If Ella were here, she'd eat her hat.

He grinned, one eyebrow sliding up. "Is that a compliment?"

"I'm not certain," she said honestly. "Your hair is unfashionably long."

"I like it that way."

She nearly agreed with him, but stopped herself. What was the matter with her? She didn't approve of his hair. Proper ladies did not find men with long hair appealing. What was he doing here?

"Allow me to escort you through the exhibit," he said offering her his arm.

She eyed him for a moment, then her curiosity got the better of her and she accepted the invitation.

"You look beautiful in that color," he said.

"Thank you. I bought this dress recently on a shopping trip with Ella. She insisted I purchase the fabric, said a gown in this color would highlight my complexion." She just repeated what he'd said. She wasn't normally such a goose. In an effort to reclaim her intelligence, she focused on the exhibit. They were walking into the piano room, her favorite place in all of London and she told him as much.

"Do you play?"

"Yes," she said, tempering her response. Rebecca had told her years ago to watch herself carefully when she spoke of music as she had a tendency to become overly excited about the subject. "I am quite fond of playing."

He eyed her for a moment before asking. "Have you seen Mr. Wilbanks lately?"

"I saw him last night, but he does not care for museums so he is not attending." She hoped that once they were married he would change his opinion of them, attend a few with her as she favored them quite a bit. She stopped walking and looked at him. "Justin, what are you doing here tonight?"

"My mother always loved music. She brought me here when I was a boy." He walked forward. "Also, I suspected you might be here."

She wanted to ask about his mother, but his admission intrigued her. "Why did you think I would be here?" They stood in front of a small Viennese piano. The keys were worn and chipped, but she longed to put her fingers upon them to hear the sweet notes.

"First you must answer a question for me." He waited until she nodded in concession. "Why is it that you are so intent on marrying George? Has he made declarations that he intends to propose?"

"Not in so many words, but he has insinuated as much." It had been two months since she'd seen or spoken to Justin, why would he seek her out with these questions about George? Perhaps he had discovered that George did, in fact, owe Rodale's money. "And we are a good match," she added with a nod.

"Someone told you that?"

She nodded again to answer his question, but kept her focus on the piano, the polished wood, the strings.

"Who?"

"People," she said dismissively.

"Your dear friend, what is her name again?"

"Ella and no." She shook her head. "Ella is not very fond of George." She nearly chuckled. That was putting it mildly. Ella did not like George at all. "He has been good friends with her brother for years. Much in the way you were with Marcus. She grew up around George so she finds him annoying, I suppose."

"Do you find me annoying?" he asked with raised brows.

She smiled. "Not at the moment."

"If not Ella, who was it that told you that George would

be a good fit for you?"

"Why are you so curious?" She eyed him for a moment. "It seems you came here to tell me something yet all you've done is ask me questions. Why the sudden interest in my relationship with George?"

He shrugged. "I don't know. Seems to me that someone important must have told you that once upon a time. I don't think he's a particularly good match for you so I'm curious as to why you do. Especially since it seems he hasn't progressed your relationships beyond weekly walks in the park and an occasional dance at a ball."

She stopped walking and looked at him. "How do you know that?"

"I've asked some questions. After he lied to you about owing me money, I made some inquires. I don't care for people associating me in their lies. I've been watching Mr. Wilbanks and his behavior at Rodale's. He still doesn't owe me any money, Chrissy. The man is a liar."

She supposed she couldn't blame him for looking into matters. In truth, George's lie bothered her as well, but she had to give him the benefit of the doubt. Certainly George had his reasons for telling her such things. Nevertheless, she didn't appreciate being on the other end of his lie either. "If I answer this question, will you tell me why you came looking for me tonight?"

"Yes."

"It was Rebecca."

"Charles's wife?"

"I wouldn't think you would remember her," she said with a smile. "Yes, she was like a mother to me, and shortly before she fell ill, we were at a party. It was my first Season and she was trying to teach me all about how to find the right sort of husband. She pointed out George, said he was handsome, polite, and he stood to inherit a title."

"Did she point any other men out that night?"

She considered for a moment, trying to bring that night to the front of her memory. Rebecca had always been so wise. Clarissa trusted her judgment above all others. "Well, yes, but I suspect she knew something about George. Could see it in his eyes perhaps. That's what she used to say about Charles. That's how she knew she would marry him. She could see it in his eyes."

Justin was quiet a few moments as they looked at the pair of harpsichords in front of them.

"Are you going to answer my question now?" she asked.

"I went to your townhome and your butler said this is where I could find you. So I came here."

"But why?"

"To see you. Is that not enough?"

She wanted to tell him that no, in fact, that was not enough, but she was too flustered to inquire further. She fell quiet again as they walked the room. They continued on until they reached the Beethoven manuscript. She stopped and stared at the parchment. The hand scrawled notes, the words beneath. The music played in her head, her hands tapped against her skirts, hitting each key perfectly. She sighed. What must it be like to have music inside of you in such a way?

They had reached the last exhibit hall. Several people poured in behind them, one of whom was a notorious gossip, the very lady who had told everyone about Clarissa's late night visit to Justin's gaming hell.

"Oh no," Clarissa said. Even though the "scandal" had been smoothed over, Clarissa was in no mood to speak to the old bitty.

"What?"

"Lady Jessup." She looked around them and saw that the end of the manuscript room was a short and darkened corridor that led to a door. She grabbed Justin's hand and pulled him quickly into the darkness. She pressed herself against the wall and pulled him to her, effectively hiding her body.

"Who is Lady Jessup?" he whispered.

"Her husband is the one who saw me at Rodale's," Clarissa explained. "If she sees me," she shook her head. "I panicked, I merely didn't wish to speak to her."

"I believe you've put yourself in an even worse situation. If you're discovered here hiding in the dark with me, you'll certainly be ruined," he said with a devilish grin.

She popped him on the arm. "Stop enjoying this. It's quite serious."

"The only way you'll be ruined is if someone sees your face."

"Well, I can't very well hide my face." She tried to look out into the exhibit hall to see if the woman was still there, but they were so far into the darkened corridor, she couldn't see.

"No, but I can." He leaned down and kissed her.

His lips were softer than she was anticipating. His hand cradled her neck, and for the briefest of moments, Clarissa forgot everything. Forgot who she was, who she was supposed to be, and most certainly where they were. Instead, she focused on the brush of his lips against hers, the tender way he held her. Her eyes fluttered closed and she clutched her hands to his arms.

He deepened the kiss and she slid her arms up around his neck, perfectly contented to be kissing here in this darkened corridor without a notion of who could be watching them.

The voices in the exhibit area faded and Justin pulled back. "I think everyone has left that hall," he said.

Clarissa blinked up at him. "Thank you."

He grinned. "You need not thank me for that."

• • •

Good heavens.

Now as she and Aunt Maureen sat in the carriage traveling home, Clarissa's knees were still a bit shaky from Justin's kiss. Maureen was rattling on about something that had occurred at the museum, but all Clarissa could think about was that kiss. Luckily no one had seen them. The room had been completely empty when they'd stepped out of the darkened corridor. Still, the thought of being caught in Justin's arms shot a thrill of excitement though her body.

Her lips still tingled. She brought a finger to them, but they didn't feel any different to the touch. Did they, perhaps, appear different? She smiled at her aunt, but the woman didn't seem to notice, merely continued talking.

She still didn't know why Justin had sought her out tonight let alone what had made him kiss her. She had never even considered that he might be tempted to do such a thing. George certainly never had. Nor had any other gentleman. Well, except for Harry Parsons, but they'd been all of seven at the time and he'd mostly just mashed his lips upon hers. It hadn't been exciting for either of them and they'd agreed on the spot to never do such a thing again.

"Clarissa, dear, did you hear me?" Aunt Maureen said.

"What?" Clarissa looked up and across the carriage to her aunt. The inside lantern lit the space and illuminated the older woman's face. She looked at Clarissa expectantly. "No, my apologies, Aunt Maureen, I'm afraid my mind was elsewhere. It was such an exhilarating exhibit. What did you say?"

Maureen's features softened. "I'm glad you enjoyed the exhibit, dear. Was the manuscript as magnificent as you expected?"

It had been and yet Beethoven's creation paled in comparison to Justin's kiss. "Indeed," was all Clarissa could manage.

"Very good. As I was saying your brother and Miss March, well, I suppose I cannot call her that now that they're married. They're coming home tomorrow. We'll be hosting a small dinner party upon their return."

"That should be nice," Clarissa said.

The kiss aside, it had been quite fortuitous seeing Justin tonight. His presence had solved one of her problems. She'd been wondering who could assist her in her charade as Mr. Bembridge and then the perfect answer had nearly fallen in her lap, as it were.

Justin Rodale.

He was a man known in social circles, even accepted, for the most part. He certainly didn't owe her any favors, but she knew she could trust him. It appeared it was once again time to pay him a visit. This time though she'd avoid any would-be scandals by not going to his gaming hell, she'd go directly to his house.

• • •

The mantle clock chimed midnight and Justin looked up for the first time in two hours. He stood, stretched his back, and walked the length of his office twice. He'd been going over the quarterly records for Rodale's since he had returned from the museum, and it would seem they had increased profits for the ninth quarter in a row. To say Rodale's was doing well was a significant understatement. He smiled. Would that his arse of a father been alive to see his success.

It had taken him some significant concentration to get his mind on the books tonight. After the kiss he'd shared with Chrissy in the museum, he couldn't get her off his mind. He kept hearing her words again and again, "thank you." He'd never had a woman thank him for kissing her before.

He definitely intended to kiss her again, until she told him to stop.

There was a pounding as someone slammed the knocker into his front door. Justin glanced at the clock again, quite late for a visitor and he couldn't recall expecting anyone. Perhaps it was his brother. Roe kept mostly nighttime hours, seeming to prefer moving about the world in the darkness. Justin's butler knocked on the study door, then opened it. "Lady Clarissa here to see you."

She entered wearing a dark cloak, the hood covering her facial features. She swept it back off her head and smiled. "Hello, Justin."

"Chrissy. This is a surprise." Justin nodded to the butler who turned and left the room. "Twice in one night, to what do I owe the pleasure?"

"Can I not simply come for a visit?"

"No, you would not do such a thing. Not after the last time you came to see me. Quite the trouble you caused." He clicked his tongue. "Come in and sit."

She came out of her cloak and laid it against one of the leather chairs, then sat in the one opposite. "Well, now that you've been established as a dear friend of the family, perhaps it's not too scandalizing. But you see right through me. I came because I need a favor."

She still wore that pink confection she'd had on earlier. Pretty, feminine, and so damned tempting. Though he had seen her a handful of times now, he still was not quite used to Clarissa as a woman. He still remembered how she'd looked as a thin girl of fifteen. Now, though, the only hint of the young girl he'd known had been her eyes. You never forgot eyes that blue. Gone were the gangly arms and legs, and in their place was a woman full of delicious curves. "More debts to pay off?"

"Not exactly."

He'd asked about George earlier that evening to see if the man had been progressing their relationship, it did not seem as if he were. Still Justin wanted to remind Clarissa of George's poorer qualities so that she might change her mind about marrying him.

"Did you ever find out the truth from Mr. Wilbanks? Why he'd lied about owing me money?"

"I never inquired. It didn't seem important."

He could tell by the flicker in her jaw that that wasn't the precise truth, but he merely nodded.

"No, this isn't about George at all, but a different matter. It would seem that my dearest friend Ella, well, her father, has made a series of poor investments and is need of some assistance."

Justin frowned. "You wish me to loan him money?"

"No, of course not. Were it that simple, we could loan them the necessary funds." She took a deep breath. "What I am about to tell you cannot leave this room. Can I trust you with my secret?" she asked, her blue eyes pierced into his.

It was on his tongue to tell her that she could trust him with anything. Anything save perhaps her virtue, as she was looking increasingly more fetching by the moment in that gown with its plunging neckline that left little to his imagination regarding her breasts. Her pale blond hair was piled intricately on her head in a display of curls and jeweled pins. "How did you get here?" he asked.

"I hired a hack. You didn't answer my question."

"Yes, you can trust me," he said. He sat, realizing he was most eager for what secret she was about to share. He'd known Chrissy since she was but a girl. He'd been schoolmates with her older brother, and Justin had spent many days over at the Kincaid family estate. But it wasn't until she'd come back into his life a couple months before that'd he'd realized what a fine and beautiful woman she'd become. He'd done his part then to ensure her reputation hadn't been irreparably damaged before he'd gone back to his days and nights at Rodale's. He'd missed her though, these past two months. Missed her lovely face and her intoxicating eyes. He couldn't deny that it had been part of why he'd decided to seek her out tonight at the museum. He could simply take the matter regarding George to Clarissa's brother, but instead Justin opted to see if he couldn't persuade her on his own. There were certain techniques he could use to get her mind off

George Wilbanks.

And he couldn't deny that kissing her proved to quite enjoyable for him as well. Before they could get to any more kissing, though, she had come here for a reason. At the moment she sat looking up at him expectedly.

"What is this secret you have, Chrissy?"

"Alright, I'm going to simply start talking so I can get all of this out before I lose my nerve. Before Marcus came home, we, Aunt Maureen and I, were struggling to deal with who had been, up until that point, our family's solicitor. He refused to have any dealings with either one of us and there was no way to know when or if Marcus would return." She let out a puff of air. "In a moment of desperation and haste I posed as a new solicitor, hired myself, so to speak, and have been managing the family coffers since then." She eyed him cautiously.

Well, that, he had not expected. "Are you telling me that you have been posing as a solicitor and making financial investments and the like for the entire Kincaid estate?"

Her chin bumped up a notch. "Indeed, I have."

"And?"

"And what?"

"How have you done?"

"Quite well. It would seem that my mind is given to such matters." She smiled broadly. "And I do enjoy it, as unladylike as that might be. 'Tis why this must be a secret. Obviously such news would ruin me for certain."

He nodded. "Yes, we mustn't allow them to know that you have a fully functioning mind. Now, then, what is it you would like me to do with said secret?"

"As I mentioned before, Ella's family is in a bit of a

situation. She asked me if I would refer our family solicitor to her father."

"She does not know the truth?"

"No, I couldn't afford to confide in her. It was bad enough that Aunt Maureen knew the truth."

He knew the girls were quite close and the fact that Clarissa was here seeking his assistance with her secret and not her dearest friend gave him pause. "You want me to pose as this solicitor?"

"Heaven's no, people know you. No, I would merely like for you to pose as another client, so to speak, make a recommendation to her father. Everyone knows you've done exceptionally well with your gaming establishment. Your finances are all in order, are they not?"

"My coffers are quite full if that's what you're asking."

"Yes, then I'm certain her father would trust your recommendation."

"And what am I to tell him of this solicitor? Why does this Mr. — ?"

"Bembridge. Mr. Ignatius F. Bembridge, LLB,"

He raised one eyebrow. "That's quite a name, you couldn't think of anything more subtle?"

She waved her hand dismissively. "Mr. Bembridge is horribly shy, prefers to do all of his correspondence through the post and telegraph. He doesn't get out much, you see," she said.

"No, of course he doesn't. And once you are secured as Ella's family's new solicitor, you will simply be making wiser investments for them?"

"Precisely."

"And what if your investments fail?"

She opened her mouth, then closed it. Her brow furrowed in a frown. "I had not considered such a notion. I've had such great success with my own investments. I suppose I could give them some of our surplus."

"Interesting thought. You've had some good fortune, you have made wise choices, but I have been doing this longer, another set of eyes to be certain. Since this is the first time you'll be using someone else's money. How about you allow me to provide you with a second opinion on their investments?"

She thought for a moment. "I suppose that makes sense." She came to her feet. "So you will do it?"

"Yes, I will meet with her father." He stepped toward her. "On one condition."

"Which is?"

"Another kiss."

Her eyes widened and her breath caught. She brought her hand to her chest. "You would like to kiss me again?"

He wanted to kiss her again and again until she was dizzy from it. "Consider it payment for my favor. And for keeping your secret, as it were. You don't want to be beholden to me, do you, Chrissy?"

She bit down on her lip.

He traced one finger down the side of her face, then moved it across her bottom lip. "Tell me, why would you want to hide the passionate woman you truly are, the woman you hide beneath all the propriety." His finger trailed down her throat.

She swallowed. "I'm not hiding behind anything."

Her pulse flickered beneath his touch and her breath came in short gasps.

"I swear, I'm a perfectly ordinary woman. Dull, really."

He chuckled. He placed feather-light kisses on her neck. "You, dear Chrissy, are anything but ordinary."

She leaned into his touch.

It was all the invitation he needed. He tilted up her chin and slashed his mouth across her. He didn't ease her into the kiss, but allowed his passion to devour her. Her hands gripped his shoulders. She met him with as much fervor as he delivered.

She wanted him.

That thought sent blood rushing to his groin. He'd never wanted a woman to want him as much as he did tonight.

Their tongues molded, stroked, grazed. Her passion was intoxicating. He wanted to pick her up, press her against the wall. Have her wrap her legs around him, but he stood his ground, merely holding her face as he kissed her deeply.

God he wanted her. And she wanted him. He let his mouth trail down the column of her milky throat. He wanted to touch her everywhere. Reach into her bodice, cup her breasts, feel her nipples harden against his palm.

He forced himself to step away from her. He couldn't have her, not really. She was far too good for him. But that didn't mean he couldn't enjoy kissing her. Perhaps in doing so he'd change her mind about marrying George Wilbanks.

Chapter Three

After the kiss, Justin had bundled Clarissa into his own carriage and sent her back to her townhome. Then he'd left and made his way to Rodale's for the evening. Her request had surprised him, as had her admission, though not nearly as much as her reaction to his kiss. He'd gotten the distinct feeling that he had not ended their embrace she would have allowed him to steal her virtue completely. As tempting as that thought was, Justin needed to be more careful with his advances. He could kiss her, but he couldn't allow things to go much further.

He'd admit that her secret had come as a surprise. Out of all the things she could have said in his study, that she'd been posing as a solicitor and making financial decisions for the Kincaid fortune had not even entered his mind. He couldn't say he was surprised that Clarissa was accomplished in such a task, she'd always been quite clever, but she also strived to be so perfectly ladylike and this was anything but. He'd agreed to assist her as much because he was fascinated by the venture as his interest in spending more time with her.

It puzzled him that she hadn't inquired more about George Wilbanks' debt and the lie the man had told her about his connection with Rodale's. Certainly she was curious about it, if not offended by the lie itself. This was a man she fully intended to marry. It didn't seem as if George was quite so certain. As far as he could tell George Wilbanks was no more interested in Clarissa than he was the handful of other pretty girls with whom he flirted and spent time.

Justin left the street and made his way inside his establishment. It was crowded tonight, not unusual, but he normally made his rounds on the gaming floor earlier in the evening, then spent the rest of the time in his office unless he was needed. Tonight he'd arrived later than usual. After working on his own books and then the spontaneous visit from Clarissa, he was only now arriving at Rodale's and it was nearing two. He nodded to Lord Asterfield who sat with a large pile of winnings in front of him. The man smiled brazenly and yelled something across the room. Justin smiled, but kept walking.

He walked over to the wager book to see if the odds had changed for Clarissa in George's marriage game. For the moment it seemed as though the other girl had a slight lead on Clarissa. Justin nodded to a few more patrons, then made his way to the stairs that led up to his offices without anyone else trying to stop him. He was not interested in conversing with these men tonight.

He stepped into his office and stared down through the windows to the floor below. All of this was his, built from nothing. Ten years ago, he'd been done with his schooling and his father had decided he'd bestowed enough generosity to his bastard son so he'd kicked Justin out just as he'd increased Roe's allowance. Justin had had nothing, save the money he'd bilked from schoolmates over the years of covert card games. Their father had died two years after that.

Now Rodale's was the most opulent and profitable gaming establishment in all of London. For most aristocrats, Justin's success wasn't enough for him to be welcomed into their ranks, not truly. They enjoyed Rodale's, jested with him, pretended as if they were friends, but on the few occasions he had attended a proper Society function many had pretended they'd never met him.

Justin stepped into the office where he and his assistant manager, Mr. Clipps, shared a space. Justin could have taken this entire area for his own office and left Clipps in the outer room, but the man knew as much about Rodale's as Justin did. And it made it easier for both to keep track of the ledgers. He dropped the ledgers he'd brought in from home onto Clipps' desk.

"We're doing well. Continuing to increase in profit," Justin said.

"I'll dig into them tonight. By the by, looks as if you might have gotten a love letter," Mr. Clipps said, nodding to the pile of post sitting on his desk. He took a bite of whatever Mrs. Clipps had packed for him that evening.

Justin inhaled. "Is that roast beef?"

The man nodded and mumbled something with his mouth full. "Want some?"

Justin was tempted, it smelled delicious and he knew Mrs. Clipps was an accomplished cook. "No." He walked over to see what letter the man was talking about. There on the desk amidst other pieces of post—mostly bank notes and the like paying off debts—sat an envelope addressed, not to Rodale's, but rather directly to Mr. Justin Rodale. The penmanship was decidedly feminine. He snatched up the envelope.

Mr. Clipps chuckled. "Expecting that one, were you?"

"No, merely curious." He'd be a liar if he said he didn't hope that this letter gave him some information about the identity of his mother. He had searched for so long, had sent out so many inquiries and followed so many leads that had, in the end, led to nothing but disappointment. But he wouldn't need to utter that hope aloud even though Clipps had been with him through most of his search.

Justin went and sat at his own desk and opened the envelope. It was an invitation to have dinner with Marcus and Vivian when they returned to London the following day. A pleasant surprise, but certainly not the one he'd been hoping for. He ignored the surge of disappointment that shuttered through him.

"So what does the lady have to say?" Mr. Clipps asked after Justin dropped the parchment onto his desk.

"It is an invitation for dinner."

Clipps' eyebrows rose. "More invitations to join into proper Society. Too bad your damned father isn't alive to see it," he said.

"Yes, too bad." He glanced back at the invitation knowing this meant he'd get to see Clarissa in a more formal setting. But it did beg the question as to whether or not Clarissa arrange for her beau to be there too?

Justin knew, though, that while George did frequent his establishment, he played billiards and the occasional game of hazard, and he was always lucky. He might have debts somewhere else, but certainly not at Rodale's.

Perhaps that was the truth. Perhaps Wilbanks gambled more heavily at a less reputable hell and he hadn't wanted to tell her the truth. Either way, Justin would wager Wilbanks never expected Clarissa to attempt to pay his debts on her own.

Over the years, even though he no longer had a connection to her family, he'd followed the gossip about Clarissa Kincaid out of curiosity. Or, more to the point, the absolute lack of gossip. Clarissa's reputation was as spotless as a chandelier at one of the Ton's parties. At least, it had been until the moment she'd stepped out of the carriage and onto the doorstep of his gaming hell. No one could have predicted she would do something so reckless. So brazen. But Vivian March, now Vivian Kincaid, had worked her particular form of magic and salvaged Clarissa's reputation. Of course, that was unless someone had seen her arrive at his townhome earlier that evening. He'd wager not, she'd kept herself pretty well hidden in that cloak.

"Clipps, I want you to find out what you can on George Wilbanks."

"Interesting," Clipps said. He absently rubbed at the thick stubble on his chin.

"In what way?"

Clipps shrugged. "I thought we were done with that issue. You see Lady Blue-eyes again?"

Justin couldn't help but smile. "I did. And she is in that wager book downstairs. If the man lied to her once, he'll likely do it again. I merely want to uncover any other secrets he might have and give her all the information possible so she can decide to marry him knowing his faults as well as his merits. I'm suspicious that he prefers to spend the bulk of his coin at a different establishment. One not as acceptable as ours."

"Probably right. There are lots of those places willing to take wagers on all manner of things."

Justin leaned back in his chair and folded his hands across his abdomen. "I want to know everything though. What he plays, who he plays with, how much he wagers, side wagers, all of it."

"Consider it done." Clipps nodded, then stood to leave.

"Have you discovered anything about the other matter I asked you to look into?" Justin asked.

Clipps rocked back on his heels. "Another dead end, I'm afraid."

Justin nodded and Clipps slipped out the door.

"Bloody hell." Another dead end. This was the third one in the last two months. His father had told him he would never discover his mother's real identity, and damned if the man hadn't been right. But Justin refused to give up. The right evidence had to be out there, he merely needed to find it. While he looked into his mother's identity, he would also do his best to ensure Chrissy was protected from making a huge mistake. Everything Justin knew about George right now indicated he was quite similar to Justin's father. Selfish and dishonest. The last thing he'd want to see is Chrissy married off to someone like that.

• • •

The following day Justin decided it was time to pay a call on his half-brother. Some days being the brother of the Duke of Chanceworth had its benefits. The man knew practically everyone in town. While Clipps was looking into what Wilbanks did outside of Rodale's, Roe might be able to give Justin information as to the man's reputation in Society.

The ride to Roe's townhome gave Justin enough time to consider the current situation. What he needed to decide was to what lengths he would go to deter Clarissa's intent to marry Wilbanks. Distracting her with kisses might only take him so far. It would seem that no matter what the plan it would require him to return once again to proper Society. Ever since Vivian had seen to it that he'd been invited to some parties a couple months before, the invitations continued to arrive. He politely sent declines, but perhaps now he should accept a few.

He glanced up at the townhome before him. Five stories of brown bricks and white arched windows. Justin owned a similar one now, but this one definitely came with memories.

He remembered being a boy in their father's house. They'd had a ball once when Justin and Roe had been home from school for some reason or another. The duke had coldly instructed Justin to stay upstairs out of sight, since he was not truly a member of their family. The duchess had been mortified, gone to Justin's defense, but her words had fallen on deaf ears. Justin had spent the evening hiding at the top of the stairs, listening to the music and the party guests laugh. He'd even seen a couple sneak into the darkened spot behind the stairs for some heated kissing.

Normally, he wouldn't bother to meet his brother here. He didn't care for the Chanceworth townhome. But, today, they had nothing set up and he needed to speak with him. He knocked and was admitted into the duke's study to wait for his brother. Justin stood in the room glancing around at all the antiquities their father had collected. The man had been particularly fond of Chinese abacuses, and so there were at least fifteen of them in all different styles and mediums.

The first time Justin had stood in this room he'd been a boy of only twelve, and his mother, or at least the woman who'd raised him, had fallen ill and brought him to live with his father. That had been the same day he'd found out that Eloise Rodale, the woman with whom he'd lived with until that moment, was not his real mother. She'd certainly treated him as a mother would treat a son, loving, yet stern when she'd needed to be.

His father hadn't been too keen on the bastard son showing up on his doorstep. The duke had been completely prepared to turn the boy out on his own, but the duchess had come in, heard the commotion and come to Justin's aid. She'd demanded her husband claim him in some capacity and Justin had been welcomed into the home, educated alongside their son, the heir, Monroe. It had taken the death of their father for Roe to be willing to accept him, and Justin couldn't say he blamed him. He'd been so damned angry with their father, he hadn't been worth being around when they were younger. It was one of the reasons he'd spent so much time at the Kincaid family's home, to be around what he'd deemed a happy family.

Roe stepped into the room. "Damnation, Rodale, how many times must I tell you not to come this bloody early in the morning?"

Roe was disheveled. There was no other word to describe him. His shirt was undone, he wore no waistcoat, and he hadn't bothered to put on shoes. Red lines cobwebbed across his eyes indicating he'd once again had an extremely late night.

Justin chuckled. "Dear brother, it is nearly noon, that hardly constitutes as being bloody early. Perhaps if you would go to sleep before sunrise you might be more amenable to the daylight hours."

Roe tossed himself down on the sofa and glared at his brother. "Yes, but it is in those late hours that the best players come out. I cannot abide to play *Vingt-et-un* with those who aren't skilled, you know that."

Justin sat in the wing-backed chair adjacent to the sofa. "Yes, I do know that. Did you win?"

He stacked his bare feet on the occasional table in front of the sofa. "Of course, I always win," Roe said with a lazy shrug. He leaned his head back and closed his eyes. "Now, to what do I owe the honor of your intrusion?"

"What do you know of George Wilbanks?" There was no need to be anything but direct when it came to communicating with his brother.

Roe cracked open one eye. "What do want with him?"

"Curiosity, Roe, humor me."

"Very well, let me see, George Wilbanks." Roe puffed out a breath. "His father, the Viscount, is older than Christ, but the man refuses to die thus leaving George to survive on a regulated allowance. The old man must be approaching eighty, yet he still thrives in Parliament."

"And George is annoyed that his father won't die?"

Roe chuckled. "I suppose he is. Honestly, I don't know George well. He doesn't play *Vingt-et-un*, prefers billiards, I believe." Roe was quiet for a moment, then nodded. "Oh, and I believe I heard once that he enjoys boxing."

"He plays billiards when he goes to Rodale's," Justin said.

"You do not offer boxing."

"True. It's a risky form of wagering. Giving them permission to beat each other in one room encourages them to do so in the other rooms." Justin shook his head. "No boxing at Rodale's."

"Of course not." Roe bracketed his hands behind his head and looked at Justin.

"Is that all you know?"

Roe tilted his head. "You know I don't pay much attention to gossip unless it is about me. That I find infinitely amusing."

"Think, Roe, people talk, especially when they play cards and drink. You must have heard something about the bloke over the years."

"Demanding this morning, aren't you? He likes women," Roe said. Then he rolled his eyes. "A lot of women."

"Does that mean he has several mistresses?"

"No, nothing like that. Don't think he could afford one mistress let alone multiple ones. I meant that he enjoys having more than one woman. I believe I heard that he has a handful of ladies he courts, makes promises to, but has no intentions to follow through with any of them."

Justin exhaled slowly. "And I'm the bastard."

"Why the interest?"

"There's a wager at Rodale's about whom he'll end up marrying. Evidently the viscount has made him an ultimatum that he must marry before the old man dies. Clarissa is on that list."

Roe's brows shot up. "Should have known this was about a skirt. You marry her first. Problem solved."

"I'm going to pretend you didn't even suggest that."

"Suit yourself, but it would get you what you want," Roe said.

Justin didn't comment. He might want Clarissa, but he could not have her.

Roe yawned, stretched his legs out in front of him. "Anything else of interest in your life right now?"

Clarissa was masquerading as a financial solicitor, but that was her secret he'd agreed to keep. Though Justin knew Roe would merely find it amusing, not scandalous. "Marcus and his new wife invited me to dinner."

Roe smiled. "I knew you wouldn't be able to stay out of Society forever. They lure you in like a worm on a hook."

"They might invite me to attend parties, but I will never be accepted as anything more than a bastard."

"Perhaps, but you are a particularly wealthy bastard and the brother of a duke. Certainly my name counts for something in your favor."

"That is doubtful," Justin said. "You are far too disagreeable, not to mention vexing and spoiled."

Roe shrugged. "I do my best. I suppose Clarissa will be at this dinner?"

"I suppose she will be there as well. The invitation did not come with a complete guest list."

"See you could begin your courtship there, make your intensions known to her brother."

"I'm certain Marcus would be thrilled with that prospect." Though Justin could argue that he himself was certainly a better choice than George Wilbanks. Still he could never court her, not with serious intentions regardless of how tempting that suggestion had been. She was a daughter of the Ton, and he would always be nothing more than the boy hiding at the top of the stairs.

• • •

Clarissa stood in front of the mirror as her maid put the finishing touches on the back of her dress. Ella burst into the room and the maid jumped, clutching her chest and muttering something in Gaelic. "Una, you may go now. Thank you." Clarissa dismissed the maid who was smiling shakily now.

"I didn't mean to frighten her," Ella said. She crossed the room and sat in one of the chairs situated in front of the window.

"She's a jumpy one, that one." Clarissa eyed her friend. "You have gossip. I can always tell when you have something you want to say because you purse your lips and smile at the same time. I've actually tried to do it in the mirror before. It's not an easy expression to make."

Ella gave her a full smile. "I do no such thing.

Clarissa joined Ella and sat in the opposite chair. "Spill it, Ella."

"Oh very well. So I overheard Victor and two other friends chatting in my dad's study. Appears there is a wager going around regarding George."

"About his father forcing him to marry. I only just heard that rumor last night," Clarissa said.

"Then you know about the wager?"

Clarissa's heart stuttered. "No, I don't believe I heard anything about that."

"Well, the good news, I don't think you have anything to be overly concerned about because Franny Cooper is, at the moment, at the top of the betting pool."

Clarissa shook her head. "Wait, you have to start over, I have no notion of what you're talking about."

"There's evidently a wager at Rodale's about which woman George will marry," Ella said.

Clarissa's heart pounded, then she remembered what Ella had said just before. "But they think his bride will be Franny Cooper?"

"Precisely."

"And why is that the good news? Ella, you know that I want to marry George."

Ella nodded slowly. "Well, I know that you have wanted that, yes, but I thought once you knew how callous he was being, allowing you to be the object of a wager, I thought you'd change your mind."

"Why ever would I do a silly thing like that?"

"Because he's obviously entertaining the idea of marrying a variety of women. Don't you find that the least bit offensive?"

She did. It hurt, especially after she'd developed such strong feelings for George and she'd thought they'd been reciprocated. "He might not have made the list himself."

"I suppose that is true." But Ella seemed unconvinced. "You and Franny Cooper are so very different though."

"I believe you must know more about her than I do." Clarissa had met the girl on a handful of occasions and she seemed friendly enough. "What is it about her that makes her so different? Other than the obvious that she's taller and thinner and more exotic looking?"

Ella's features scrunched. "She's more worldly, brazen, bold. My mother's friends find her a vastly interesting bit of conversation. They're always exchanging stories about some of Franny's behavior. There are rumors that she enjoys men stealing kisses in the moonlight, but as far as I know no one has caught her."

"So it's all speculation," Clarissa said.

"I suppose, but you've seen her, the dresses she wears. She's certainly more brazen than either one of us."

Brazen and worldly. Perhaps that was why George hadn't yet proposed to her.

"We should probably get downstairs for the dinner party," Ella said. "I only wanted to discuss this with you beforehand. Though the conversation didn't exactly go the way I'd planned."

"Ella, you'll still love me and be my dearest friend if I become George's wife, won't you?"

Ella smiled warmly. "Of course."

"You go ahead, I'll be down in just a moment." Ella left her alone and once again Clarissa stood in front of the mirror. The dress did accent her curves nicely, but the blond ringlets clashed with her womanly figure. There was nothing brazen or worldly about her.

She'd certainly felt both of those things in Justin's arms, while he'd kissed her, while she'd kissed him back without thought to how her behavior might be perceived. Her dear, late sister-in-law, Rebecca, would no-doubt have been horrified by that, but it had been a different time when she'd met and married Charles. Things were different now, women needed more than a big dowry to catch a man's eye. Perhaps it was time for Clarissa to start thinking about how she could get George's attention for good. She might not know how to be worldly and brazen, but she was a quick study.

Chapter Four

Justin was shown into the parlor at the Kincaid townhouse. Marcus and his new wife, Vivian, stood in the room conversing with Marcus's cousins and a young woman whom Justin did not know. Immediately, Vivian stepped over to him. Marcus followed behind her after patting some older gentleman on the shoulder.

"Mr. Rodale," Vivian said. "I'm so pleased you could come tonight."

"We are friends now. You must call me Justin." He shook Marcus's hand. In the world he'd grown up in, full of the wealthy and titled who always found a reason to disparage him, Justin had always trusted Marcus. "Welcome back from your honeymoon. I will not inquire as to how it went."

Vivian blushed and Marcus smiled broadly. He grabbed his wife around the waist and pulled her to him. "It was a lovely break from London," Vivian said. "I am glad to be back though."

"Pleased my sister didn't get herself into any more trouble in our absence," Marcus said as Clarissa entered the room. She caught Justin's gaze and her steps faltered. Evidently she hadn't known he'd been invited.

Clarissa was radiant in a bright yellow dress that accented her golden hair. The gown fit her perfectly, molding to her curves. It had only been the night before that those curves had been pressed against him, her sultry mouth pressed to his.

Justin swallowed. Perhaps she hadn't gotten herself into trouble, but only because she hadn't been caught going to his townhome. And because no one had seen them kissing at the museum. Now Justin was the one making an ass of himself. He had no business looking at Clarissa in such a way, let alone while her older brother and his dear friend, stood next to him. Thankfully Marcus could not read his carnal thoughts.

"Justin, I did not realize you'd been invited to our family dinner," Clarissa said.

"Clarissa, where is Maureen?" Vivian asked, saving Justin from having to respond to Clarissa's quip.

"She said she was not feeling very well and for us to send up a tray," Clarissa said. She went and stood by the other young woman and the girls put their heads together, whispering.

"Then let us not delay dinner any further," Marcus said.

"If I could have a moment with Clarissa," Justin said.

Marcus nodded, then led the rest into the dining room. Vivian busied herself directing people to the appropriate chairs.

Clarissa's friend eyed her, then gave her a smile and

stepped into the dining room.

When they were alone, Justin spoke first. "Is that Ella?"

"It is. Did you have a chance to speak with her father?" Clarissa asked in a hushed voice.

"I visited Lord Weaver this morning."

She twisted her pinky finger with her other hand. "And?"

"I told him that you and I had spoken about the matter based on a conversation you and his daughter had. He was reluctant at first, but I convinced him that Mr. Bembridge was an excellent solicitor and would be able to restore his coffers. He's agreed. You should be receiving the letter hiring," he cleared his throat, "Mr. Bembridge in the next day or so."

She gave him with a brilliant smile. "I could hug you right now, Justin. Thank you for helping. I couldn't live with myself if I knew my dearest friend's family was in dire straits and I could have helped, but stood by and did nothing."

"I should very much enjoy that hug, I believe, but perhaps we should keep our embraces more of the private nature. Do you have ideas for their investments?"

"I do." She told him about her thoughts and he was pleased that she'd already thought about several investments that would be highly profitable.

"Good ideas. I think those are excellent choices. I have a few other suggestions you can look at as well," he said. "If you need additional options."

"This makes us partners, Chrissy," he whispered next to her ear. "Shall we?" He offered his arm and she took it. They walked into the dining room.

He smiled when he realized they'd seated him next to Clarissa. She, on the other hand, seemed somewhat flustered, but she took her seat nonetheless, refusing his assistance when he offered. Her friend was seated on the other side of her and was more than pleased when he offered her help. She smiled broadly up at him. She was shorter than Clarissa, more plump as well, and she was very pretty. Pretty in a fresh, straight from the schoolroom sort of way with her bouncing brown curls and wide green eyes.

"Justin, I am so pleased you could make it this evening," Vivian said. "I didn't know what your schedule would be, but I don't suppose your establishment begins to get too busy until dinner parties like these come to a close."

"We do tend to get busier afterwards, but there is always gaming to be found at Rodale's. We are open whenever someone wants to play."

"Fascinating," Vivian said. "I've never been much of a gambler myself, but it is interesting."

• • •

Clarissa didn't find it interesting in the least. Wasting money on a game of chance made no sense to her at all. And truly all she could think of was the rumor Ella had shared with her. Obviously Clarissa had some brazenness inside her as Justin had been able to coax it out with merely a kiss. Of course it had been a toe-curling, knee-weakening kiss that certainly would have caused even her majesty to show a little wantonness.

"I am not a gambler either," Justin said.

Ironic, that—Justin owning a gaming establishment, but not choosing to gamble with his own money. George was obviously a gambler, or perhaps he had lied about owing money all together. Understanding more about all of that, despite her disinterest, could make her more worldly, couldn't it?

"Perhaps merely a shrewd businessman," Vivian said.

"I made some good guesses on what would be popular with this crowd. While I am not one of them," he said, "I was raised alongside them and I know them fairly well."

"It's amazing what you can learn simply by watching," Vivian said.

"Indeed." Justin turned his heated gaze to her. "You look lovely tonight, Chrissy," he said with a grin.

Though he did not touch her, warmth radiated off his hands and seemed to permeate through her evening gown. She shook off a shiver. "Sh! Someone could hear you."

"Hear me give a beautiful woman a compliment? Is that such a sin?"

He had her there. She nodded in concession. "Thank you." But she refused to tell him that he too looked beautiful. Women didn't say such things regardless of the fact that for Justin Rodale it would have been the complete truth. It was ridiculous how handsome he was, with his dark features and sultry eyes. Eyes that at the very moment were staring directly at her. Precisely what was the purpose for a man to have such long eyelashes? Thick and dark, they framed his eyes, eyes so dark they were beyond brown. She shivered again.

Why was she so annoyed that he was here? She liked him, he was a family friend. She enjoyed his kisses, though certainly that would not happen again. Still, there was no reason to be irritated with him simply because she was frustrated with her recent discovery of being in a bridal competition with Franny Cooper. Clarissa smiled warmly. "Thank you for coming to welcome back my brother and his bride," she said louder than was necessary.

He nodded. "I came only to see you," he said in a low voice.

She schooled her features not giving in to the shock of his admission. Ella jabbed her elbow into Clarissa's side. She yelped, and smiled awkwardly to the rest of the table. "Hiccups," she said. Then she leaned closer to her friend. "What?" she whispered.

"Oh good heavens, Clarissa, you never told me he was so very handsome," Ella said dreamily.

"It didn't seem important."

"He's so handsome," Ella said. She leaned forward and smiled at Justin seated on the other side of Clarissa, then leaned back. "I know you said he looked like a pirate, but I was expecting him to be dirty and hairier. But he does, in fact, look like a pirate. As if he could swing down from a mast and take the helm."

It was Clarissa's turn to jab her elbow in Ella's side. "You cannot lean forward in such a way, he'll know you're staring." What was it about him that made one think of a swashbuckler? She positioned herself so that her body blocked the two people on either side of her from seeing one another. "I don't want him to think we're talking about him."

"But we are talking about him," Ella said. She looked at Clarissa with a frown.

Clarissa's heart thundered in her chest. It occurred to her, with alarming clarity, that one of the reasons she found it so distressing that he was here was because the very last time she'd seen him, he'd kissed her. She felt her cheeks grow warm and knew a blush stained her face. Thankfully the soup course was served and she had something she could focus on besides reliving that kiss again and again. Not that she hadn't already done so.

"He's really dashing," Ella whispered again. "Honestly, Clarissa, look at him"

"I will not. I am quite aware of how handsome he is. *If* you find men such as him attractive. Which I do not."

Ella held up her hand. "Clarissa, I swear, if you say anything about George, I will vomit in my purse."

"George is very handsome."

"No one ever argued that point, but you are wasting your time on him. That man is never going to marry you. Good heavens, you've been waiting for him to propose for nearly three years. And now we find out there are at handful of other women who have been waiting right along with you. You should be furious."

Clarissa wanted to argue, wanted to say that George would in fact propose. But she didn't know what to believe anymore. "Let us not fight about this again. You and I see George very differently." She wasn't even so certain she wanted to marry George, but she knew that was who Rebecca had chosen for her. Rebecca had impeccable taste. Clarissa, on the other hand, was known for making questionable judgments. Like when she'd fallen for Christopher Reynolds, she'd been so smitten, Rebecca had told her he wasn't to be trusted. She'd learned that the hard way when he'd deserted her and stolen several pieces of her jewelry.

"I thought you should know I'm looking into Mr. Wilbanks' claims of owing me money." Clarissa nearly choked as she swallowed her soup. "Do you mean to tell me that you were mistaken and that he does, in fact, owe you money?" she whispered.

He shook his head. "No, I was not mistaken. He does not owe me anything. I am merely looking deeper into the situation. I should like to know whom he does owe money, if in fact any part of his story was true."

It was on her tongue to argue that point, to tell him that George Wilbanks was an honest man, but the words died in her mouth. Clearly George had not been honest. About his debt and about his intentions towards her. He might have a perfectly reasonable reason for lying to her, but that remained to be seen. She couldn't very well praise his virtues when he'd so blatantly lied. What would Justin discover in his investigation of the matter?

"Will you tell me?" she asked.

"Tell you what?"

"Whatever you discover about George or this situation, will you give me the details?"

He nodded. "I will."

The second course was served and while that occurred, Ella leaned close to Clarissa's other ear. "Now tell me more about Mr. Rodale."

"There is nothing to tell. He is a friend of the family," Clarissa said, but even she wasn't so convinced by the words.

"I wish he were a friend of my family."

• • •

After dinner they retired to the parlor and Vivian invited Clarissa to play the harpsichord. Clarissa took a seat at the instrument. Justin stood against the wall, behind the chair where Clarissa had been sitting. He watched her as she splayed her fingers across the keys. She began to play. Her body moved over the keys and the music that poured from her fingers was sheer perfection. Her eyes closed and she felt each note of the piece. Mozart, if he wasn't mistaken. She pretended as if passion was beneath her, as if feeling strongly was something only the lower classes felt, but he could see right here, right now, in front of everyone that she was passionate about music.

He smiled. It was a starting point.

She continued playing, the notes surrounded the room and no one spoke, everyone watched her, raptly attentive to her playing. Her long fingers nimbly moved against the keys quickly and she leaned forward chewing on her lip. Ladies were supposed to sit straight and play for the entertainment of those in the room. But Clarissa played for herself, Justin could clearly see that, because she loved the music, she felt it. Now he understood why she'd looked longingly at some of the displays at the museum the other night.

Finally the song came to an end and the small room burst with applause, which brought forth a most brilliant smile from Clarissa.

Marcus's cousins stood and said their goodbyes.

Clarissa returned to her seat and Justin nodded to her.

"You play beautifully," he leaned in and whispered.

"Thank you."

"Passionately."

She whipped her head around to focus on him. She opened her mouth to say something, but words seemed to fail her.

"Merely an observation," he said with a shrug.

"Yes, well you do not need to say every thought that enters your head."

He let his gaze wander to her bosom for several breaths, watching her breasts rise and fall, then he slowly looked back at her face. "Believe me when I tell you I do not say every thought in my head."

She said nothing in return, but the rapid rise and fall of her breasts as her breathing sped said enough.

"Mr. Rodale, a word if you don't mind," Vivian said.

"Clarissa, it's been a pleasure." He bent over her hand, but did not kiss it. Then he turned and followed Vivian into the corridor. "Is there a problem?"

"No, no of course not. I merely wanted to discuss something with you. You are well aware of my, well, that is to say you know of the ways in which I can assist people," Vivian said.

"I was under the impression that when you married Marcus you had ceased the life of The Paragon," Justin said. Just months before she had been known as such in London. A woman families could go to in the midst of scandal and she would devise a plan to bury said scandal beneath the proverbial rug. She had done so for Clarissa.

Vivian smiled. "Yes, I had intended that once the truth about my past was revealed that no one would seek my services again. But it would seem that I was incorrect in that estimate."

"You have a new client, then?"

"It would seem so. Perhaps not as tricky a situation as I've handled in the past, but a puzzle to be solved nonetheless. The mother of a young woman has sought my assistance in a predicament. Her daughter does not garner the attention of men."

Justin frowned. "My apologies, Vivian, but what does this have to do with me?"

"Yes, I was just getting to that part. You were so very helpful with the situation with Clarissa, reintroducing yourself into Society to be seen publically with her and Marcus. Your presence made it all the more believable that her little visit to your establishment was nothing more than a personal invitation, even if poorly thought out. In any case, I was telling Marcus that all this girl needs is for a man to show interest in her. Some men simply need permission, if you will, from another man that declares that a woman is desirable."

"I'm still not following."

"I want you to court her."

"I beg your pardon?"

"Of course it wouldn't be a real courtship, she would know your intentions were not sincere. You would merely appear to be courting her so that perhaps another man would step forward and take an interest in her."

"You think this would work?" Justin asked. "I'm not exactly a mother's wish for her daughter."

"Nonsense," Vivian said with a pat on his arm. "You are a devilishly charming man."

Justin smiled. "Be that as it may, I'm not certain that my attentions will be all that welcomed. Who is the girl?

"Her name is Betsy Riverton." Vivian's mouth twitched. "She's not unattractive at all though I don't know that we could consider her a beauty. I believe her issue stems more from being overly talkative."

"Ah, yes, well affluent men are not known for being

attracted to women with opinions. I shall consider it."

. . .

The following day Clarissa met Ella for luncheon. They'd decided to do so with a picnic in the park. Aunt Maureen sat on a bench reading a book somewhere near them. Clarissa set out the food, cheeses and fruit with bread. It was awkward being around Ella in a way it never had been before. There was much she couldn't tell her, and Clarissa simply wasn't used to not being able to share everything with Ella.

Even when it came to George, a point they vehemently disagreed upon, yet Clarissa had always been honest with Ella. Until now. Until Clarissa had become Mr. Bembridge and kissed Justin Rodale.

Ella cleared her throat when Clarissa looked up at her, and she widened her eyes. "Are you going to tell me what's troubling you? Honestly, Clarissa, I'm your very closest friend, I shouldn't have to ask." Then Ella winced. "It's everything I told you last night, isn't it? Should I have not told you? I thought you'd want to know," she put her hand to her chest. "If it were me, I know I'd want to know if the man I thought I was going to marry had been creating a pool of women to select from."

"Of course you should have told me. I'm not upset with you in the least. Merely been considering all my options, as it were."

"Will you share them with me?"

"You shouldn't have to ask." She knew she couldn't tell Ella the truth about Mr. Bembridge, but she could include her in other matters. The fact was she needed the counsel, could use a second opinion. She looked around to make certain no one was in earshot, especially her aunt. "Mr. Rodale kissed me," she whispered.

Ella smiled broadly. "He is so handsome." She clapped her hands together. "Oh you must tell me everything. Every detail. Was it last night? When he asked to speak to you before dinner? Oh goodness, how could you have even concentrated on your food?"

"No, no, not last night. It was before."

Ella giggled. "Tell me all about it."

Clarissa smiled in return; she couldn't help it. The fact of the matter was, she very much enjoyed Justin's kiss, and to finally be able to share that with someone was exceedingly liberating. "It is hard to describe. It was very nice," she said, knowing that would never satisfy Ella, but not knowing how else to say it.

"Very nice." Ella shook her head, her curls bounced as she did. "No, porridge, when it is the right temperature and sweetened with enough honey, is very nice. Kisses from devilishly handsome men, they are more than nice. And judging from that smile on your face, I'd say it was definitely more than nice."

Clarissa nodded. "Oh, Ella, I had no notion it could be that way between a man and a woman. He is gentle, yet demanding and passionate, and oh dear heavens—" She brought a hand to her chest. "It simply curls my toes."

Ella clapped again. "I knew it! Your reaction curled my toes! Men like Mr. Rodale know all of those secrets."

"What secrets?"

Ella looked around them, then leaned close to speak in a whisper. "About the sins of the flesh. Sensual things."

Ella nodded with confidence as if she were the foremost authority on the subject. "You can tell that about him, the way he carries himself." She rubbed at her arms. "I simply can't imagine. I'm positively green with jealousy. If you want to teach yourself to be more worldly so you can compete with Franny, you need not look any further than Mr. Rodale for an excellent teacher. I wonder if we could take a joint class."

Clarissa nudged Ella with her elbow. "Be serious." But her friend's words, though spoken in jest, might be precisely what Clarissa needed.

"If Mr. Rodale looked at me the way he looked at you, I would find a way to sneak him into the darkest corner I could find," Ella said. "As often as I could."

"Ella Atkins! You would do no such thing." Clarissa's cheeks flamed. "And he looks at me no differently than he does anyone. There is a problem though."

"How could that present a problem?"

"George," Clarissa said. She took a bite of cheese and waited for the inevitable of what Ella would say. Her friend made no secret of how she felt about George, but she also was quite good at giving advice once you allowed her to spout off a little.

"Oh, Clarissa, you know how I feel about this," Ella said. Then she made a sound of derision. "That man parades around this town as if he deserved every woman in his path." She shook her head in disgust. "He certainly doesn't deserve you."

"He has to maintain appearances, but those other girls don't mean anything to him. He's told me as much." But as she said the words, doubt reared its head inside her. He had such that about the other girls months ago when she'd asked about one girl in particular. Since then he had lied to her about his debt. Perhaps he also lied about those other women, perhaps he had lied about her to other women. A shiver of revulsion pulsed through her.

"The man hasn't proposed yet," Ella said gently. "The only reason he's even considering marriage right now is this ultimatum from his father."

"He has said as much?" George had certainly talked about his father to her, but he'd never said that he hadn't wanted to marry, merely that'd he'd been waiting for the appropriate time.

"Not to me, but Clifton has mentioned it, about how George claims he never wants to marry, he wants to be free to do as he pleases. But you know my brother is sweet on you though." She waved her hand. "As much as I'd love to have you as a sister, I wouldn't suggest marrying my brother. He's such a bore. In any case, continue about George."

If George had told Ella's brother—his closest friend— that he had no intention of marrying...that was different than anything he'd told Clarissa. He was clearly lying to one of them. Or perhaps he merely said as much to his friend so that he didn't appear besotted. She took a deep breath. "He has never kissed me. And I believe that might be why he hasn't proposed, because he perceives me as being too proper, too ladylike for him to kiss," Clarissa said. "I think he cannot imagine me in the bedroom, performing wifely duties. It must be why Franny has better odds than I do right now."

"That is poppycock," Ella said.

But Clarissa wasn't so certain. George was always the

perfect gentleman with her, but she knew men had urges, desires. She knew men, men besides Justin Rodale, stole kisses from women in darkened corners and behind potted plants. George had certainly had the opportunity, but his lips had never so much as brushed the skin of her cheek.

"It is a natural concern. I do not even know if George finds me desirable," Clarissa said.

"And you want to know if kissing feels the same with him as it does with Mr. Rodale." Ella shook her head. "If I had to wager, I'd say it won't because, though George is quite handsome, he's too, I don't know, arrogant and selfish to be passionate."

"George is very handsome." Clarissa could see him in her mind, his blond hair, which oddly enough, now seemed too short. He did have a wonderful smile with deep dimples creasing his cheeks. Yet, the smile had lost its effect as of late. Ever since she learned he'd lied to her.

"Ridiculously handsome when he smiles," Ella said. She chewed on a piece of cheese, then nodded. "The way I see it, there's only one thing for you to do. You must kiss him."

"George?" Clarissa asked.

"Precisely." Ella grinned "Unless you'd prefer to kiss Mr. Rodale again."

"No, of course not," Clarissa said. She really must stop lying to Ella, but honestly she couldn't very well admit to such a thing. It was one thing to want a man you would marry to see you as brazen, quite another for her to parade her wares through London. "I have every intention of marrying George." But even as she said the words they felt false to her. She'd spent so much of her life pursuing marriage with him, was she only doing so now because without George she had no other prospects in her life? Justin certainly hadn't indicated he was interested in being more to her than he currently was. "I'm not intending to spread my favors, as it were, to the rest of the gentlemen in London. Regardless of how delicious their kisses are."

Ella thought a minute. "I'm not certain it's a solid argument, but I'll let it pass. So how shall you do it?"

"Do what?"

"Kiss George?"

"Oh, right." Clarissa considered her options for a moment. "Well, I suppose I could find a moment when we're alone and do it then."

"Tonight. At the ball. They have a fabulous garden. It would be the perfect place to sneak away and steal a kiss," Ella said.

"How do you know all of this?"

Ella shrugged. "I listen to other people's conversations. And, well, you know my mother is a terrible gossip." She grabbed Clarissa's hand. "Regretfully, it's not because anyone has been stealing my kisses."

Clarissa kissed her friend's hand. "It's only because they have not realized how wonderful you are. Someday, Ella, some man is going to come to his senses and steal all of your kisses."

Chapter Five

That evening Clarissa had asked George to take her on a walk to see the famed Brookfield gardens. He'd been somewhat reluctant, but she told him that her brother was otherwise occupied and she certainly couldn't walk there alone, so he'd agreed. As they walked quietly beside one another now Clarissa felt the nerves intensify in her stomach. She took a deep breath. She could do this. In all truth, her reputation should already be in tatters, so whatever happened tonight shouldn't make her anxious at all. And now she had some experience. She'd kissed Justin. Twice. Certainly that counted for something.

"The weather is mild this evening," George said.

"Yes. It's rather nice, almost like springtime."

They wove into the gardens that weren't quite a maze, but were windier than a typical garden. And were she here to truly enjoy the botanicals, she would have been impressed. The garden was spectacular. The sweet scent of lilac wafted through the air. There must have been thousands of candles that lit the area around the garden, making it look more like the hideaway of a fairies rather than a garden in the midst of London. There was a slight chill in the air, and the breeze ruffled across her bare arms leaving gooseflesh in its wake. They reached the area filled with several different types of roses. Pink, white, red and yellow, the small blooms surrounded Clarissa and George, the flowers' heady scent floated on the evening breeze. These roses were said to be Lord Brookfield's passion.

"It's lovely," she said.

"Indeed."

"George. You know how favorably I see you."

Favorably? That was how one spoke of their favorite soup, not the man they loved. She looked up into his handsome face. He still looked the same to her as he had always looked, yet something was different now. She knew that. But this was the man Rebecca had chosen for her, she certainly shouldn't rely on her own choices. Those had almost always gotten her into trouble.

Ella had said George had not wanted to marry. George had told her, though, on more than one occasion, that if only he could marry her. He'd always said in a playful manner, which Clarissa had interpreted as genteel flirting. Had she misread his attention all this time?

His eyebrows rose and then he shook his head with a little grin.

She should say something else, but perhaps words weren't the best indicator. She should kiss him.

Without thinking too much on the logistics of such an act, she went up on her tiptoes and kissed him. Her hands were splayed on his chest and her lips pressed against his. Initially, he didn't react, didn't kiss back, merely stood there. But then one arm slid around her waist, he pulled her abruptly to him and he kissed her, the way a man kissed a woman. The way Justin had kissed her.

Only something was different. Something was missing.

His lips were warm and there was definitely passion. Or perhaps urgency. He pressed himself against her. Something in the kiss shifted. She'd lost control and now George was kissing her. Really and truly kissing her. She should be pleased, but instead she felt something alarmingly akin to panic.

She pushed at his chest and took a step back. She was clearly not accomplished enough to feign worldliness.

His eyes had darkened and he merely stared at her. "Clarissa, my apologies. I don't know what came over me," he said. Then he turned and walked away.

Well, that hadn't gone at all the way it was supposed to. And now she was left alone in the garden. Why had the kiss felt so different than Justin's? Obviously she had done something horribly wrong.

$$\cdots$$

Justin looked over at his brother who currently lined up his cue, then shot. The balls scattered across the table, two falling into pockets. Roe had shown up at Justin's townhome earlier looking for a warm meal and a game of billiards before they both headed out to Rodale's for the evening.

Roe looked up over the table. "Have you considered finding a woman to court while you're out and about, milling with Society, as it were?" He shot again, this time he missed.

"Not particularly." He nodded toward his brother. "I'm not the one who needs an heir."

"A fact my mother reminds me of every time I see her," Roe said. "She's ready to be a grandmother." Then he leveled a gaze at Justin. "Don't think you won't hear it from her too when she sees you next. She always has thought of you as her other son."

"She's a good woman," Justin said.

"I still think it could be entertaining if you ruffled some feathers," Roe said with a laugh.

Justin lined up his own cue. "It's funny you should mention that."

"Why is that?" Roe stood up straight.

Justin shot again. "The dinner at the Kincaid's last night. Vivian approached me before I left and made me a most interesting proposition."

"Sounds positively scandalous," Roe said. It was his turn to shoot. "What did she ask?"

"I know you are aware of the type of work Vivian does for people. She was approached by a concerned mother whose daughter isn't being courted. At all. Marcus suggested that all the girl needed was one suitor and it would give other men permission to pursue her. Do you think that's true?"

Roe took another shot. He made a non-committal noise. "Perhaps. I can't say that I ever take much note of what bloke is dancing with what chit."

"You don't attend many balls."

"I attend plenty." Roe set up the table for another game of billiards. "Two a month is about all I can stand. So are you going to do it?"

"Unlike Vivian, I'm unconvinced that my courting her will solve her problems. It's likely to create new ones."

Roe took a healthy sip of his brandy. "It sounds like a good way to bring attention to the girl, even if it merely angers people that you would dare court one of their darlings. I think Vivian's right. You paying attention to the girl can only help her."

"You know I'm not going to court some girl simply to irritate the powers that be," Justin said.

"We should have traded places years ago," Roe said.

• • •

Roe and Justin finished their game of billiards and were heading to the door, deciding to simply ride to Rodale's together when Justin's butler stepped into the room.

"Lady Clarissa is here to see you," he said.

Roe waggled his eyebrows at Justin. And then Clarissa stepped into the room.

"Justin, I needed to—" she stopped short when she caught sight of Roe. "Oh your grace, I did not realize you were here. My apologies."

"No need, Lady Clarissa." Roe, in a rare show of chivalry, strode over to her and bent low over her hand for a moment before flashing her a smile. "I was on my way out. If you'll excuse me." He nodded to Justin with a wink, then left the room.

"I didn't mean to intrude," Clarissa said after Roe was out of earshot.

"You didn't. That is a rather fetching gown." The blue dress molded to her body, her décolletage was accented with fine white lace, but her cleavage was all he really noticed. He preferred looking at her rather magnificent cleavage. While far from being the only feature that contributed to her beauty—her eyes, for example, were an arresting shade of blue and her lush lips were equally enticing—her bosom was the one feature he could admire while pretending it wasn't wholly inappropriate for him to do so. No, when he looked in her eyes—indeed anywhere in the region of her face—he couldn't help but remember that Clarissa was not meant for the likes of him. "These visits of yours are becoming quite regular."

"And you find that…irritating?"

"Quite the contrary. I rather enjoy your company." He enjoyed it too much. That was the problem. Hiding a sigh, he crossed back to his decanter and poured himself a fresh glass of scotch.

"I wanted to let you know that I had received the letter of employment from Ella's father. Thank you again."

"You already thanked me for that." He eyed her a moment noting the way she bit down on her bottom lip. Yes, it was much easier to simply admire her cleavage. He took a sizable gulp of the scotch. "Is there another reason why you came?"

She exhaled slowly, clenching her gloved fingers several times before blurting out, "What do you know of the wager involving George's, well, his marital situation?"

He paused in the act of raising his glass to his lips again. "Who told you?"

"Ella. She overheard her brother and some other men talking about it." She took a few steps further into the room, placed her hands on the back of a carved mahogany chair.

"Obviously, you know about it since the betting is taking place in your establishment."

He nodded, raised the glass the rest of the way to his mouth and downed it. "Are you angry?"

Her chin bumped up a notch and defiance flashed in her eyes. "Of course not. I know that gentlemen are fond of many kinds of wagers." She hesitated then, and he noticed the way her fingertips strained against the wood where she gripped it. "I was told that I was not favored to be the bride."

"It is generally between you and another woman."

"Franny Cooper. I had not realized I had such stiff competition for George's heart."

"And you are still convinced you wish to win his heart?"

She shot him an odd look before giving her head a little shake. "You know I am. But how can I possibly win against a girl like her?"

"I have no notion of who she is." Justin allowed his gaze to take in Clarissa's figure before him. "I can assure you, though, there is no competition."

Blush reddened her cheeks. "Franny is very worldly. At least that is what I'm told. And you know who she is, remember you met her at the Welbrook ball a couple months back. She was the tall one with the dark hair, very friendly."

Justin scraped his memory and recalled the woman she spoke of. If it was the same one, she was very pretty, but held no real appeal for him compared to Clarissa.

"What do you suppose that means, her being worldly?"

Clarissa shrugged, her feminine shoulders pushed upwards ever so slightly. "She drinks brandy, perhaps curses, enjoys stolen kisses. I honestly couldn't say."

Justin smiled at her. "If only you knew how very

charming you are. So you came to me for some brandy? I'm afraid you'll be disappointed as I prefer scotch, but you're welcomed to have a glass."

Some of the tension went out of her shoulders at his teasing. "No, I was hoping you'd teach me to curse," she said with a grin.

"Yes, an interesting choice in the scheme of worldly behavior."

She laughed, then the smile faded and she shook her head.

"You shouldn't try to be someone else to persuade George to marry you." He moved to her, ran a hand down the bare skin exposed between her cap sleeve and elbow-length gloves.

"But you could teach me," she said, her voice barely more than a whisper.

"Teach you what, precisely?"

"How to be more worldly, more, I don't know, more sensual." She bit her lip again and looked up at him.

"You are not concerned about your virtue?"

"Are you planning to ravish me?"

He gripped her arm, resisting the urge to do precisely that. She would never ask such a question if she had any idea the kinds of thoughts he'd been entertaining since she'd walked into the room. Thoughts of stripping off her lovely clothes and doing sinful things to her body. Of showing her all the sinful things she could do to his. He could take her three different ways on the rug alone. "Only if you want me to."

"Perhaps merely some kissing." Again a bite of her lip.

Only kissing? Ah, if only she knew how much latitude that gave him. He was ready to nibble his way around her body.

The thought was only too tempting. Unfortunately, she would then be ruined and he'd have disgraced the sister of one of the few men in London whose opinion he actually valued. No. That wouldn't do at all.

"Tell me something," he said. "Do you believe Miss Franny Cooper kisses a great deal of men?"

Her eyes widened slightly. "I don't know, to be honest."

"Why is it you believe her to be so worldly? Has she ruined her own reputation?"

"No, she hasn't." Clarissa gave her foot a little stamp, one that was barely visible beneath the hem of her gown. "That is precisely the issue. Miss Cooper's reputation is intact. Above reproach even. And yet, somehow, she is courted by so many men. And they all seem enchanted by her."

"If she is courted by many men, perhaps you have nothing to worry about."

Clarissa seemed to consider the matter, but then she shook her head. "No. George is the most eligible of men. He is handsome, charming, titled. No girl would say no if he asked. Indeed, I am sure that merely knowing George is interested in her will convince Miss Cooper from even considering the attentions of other men."

"Indeed. George is a lucky man."

Lucky—that is—that he wasn't there in the room with Justin at that moment, for Justin would have been sorely tempted to beat this *dandy* to a bloody pulp.

"So you believe George will propose to Miss Cooper merely because she is more worldly than you?"

"It is highly likely, yes."

"I remember this Miss Cooper, I believe. You are far

lovelier."

However Clarissa merely waved away his complement. "Pretty words mean nothing in the face of Franny Cooper's charms and experiences. The very fact that she's been courted by so many men gives her an advantage I couldn't hope to match."

"But surely you have been courted by just as many men."

In expression flickered across Clarissa's face. One he couldn't quite read. Surprise maybe, as if she had revealed something she didn't mean to. Then she smiled too brightly and turned away from him, once again twisting her fingers into knots. "Why, yes. Of course. I've had many suitors. So many I barely remember their names."

If it hadn't been for that flicker of emotion, he might have accepted her words at face value. However, her obvious discomfort made it all too easy to question her explanation. He had assumed that a girl as lovely as Clarissa would have plenty of suitors, but what if he was wrong? After all, she had lost several family members when she was younger, not long after she would have had her coming out, if he was not mistaken. She would have been in mourning for a full year after the death of her sister-in-law. Add in more time for her brother's death, and she simply hadn't had much opportunity to be courted.

"Clarissa," he coaxed.

"Very well." She spun back around, her eyes flashing with chagrin. "I've had only one serious suitor other than George. His name was Christopher and I was enchanted by him, thought for certain I would marry him. He did not turn out to be the man I thought him to be. Rebecca hadn't liked him from the beginning, had warned me not to trust him, but I hadn't listened. It was all very long ago. So do you see? Do you understand now why I am so worried George might have his head turned by Miss Cooper?"

Indeed he did. Then again, he had understood all along that George was not the sort of man for Clarissa. The man was not the gentleman she believed him to be. However, he couldn't bring himself to disillusion her, not when she had come to him for help. Not when she was so clearly—and adorably—worried.

"Let's discuss courtship. Perhaps if you are a bit more comfortable being wooed you will not worry so."

Her eyes widened. "You intend to court me?"

He waited for her to have a more telling reaction. Would she be accepting of such a gesture from him? He doubted it. But if he could busy her, occupy her mind enough that perhaps George did decide to propose to Franny Cooper, then Justin would feel as if he'd done his duty to Clarissa. And done it without devouring her body. "No, I meant only that we could set up scenarios."

"Oh, like in a play?"

"Precisely." He took her hand and pulled her over to the settee near the fireplace. "What do men do these days to court women?"

"A myriad of things. Picnics, walk in the park, rides in the park, poetry—"

"Poetry. Yes, that is somewhere to start. Now would this be poems that the gentleman himself wrote? For instance, I could compare your fair hair to that of freshly pulled wheat. Then I could liken your lovely complexion to the finest quality alabaster. Your eyes, though, those would be far more difficult. The color is so very unique, not quite the color of the sky on a bright spring day, nor the color of the ocean off of Plymouth's coast. It is rather like a color that only an artist could create by blending and mixing the most beautiful shades of blue."

The expression on Clarissa's face filled with surprise and something sharply akin to awe. He simultaneously wanted to embrace her and chuckle. "Or perhaps it's more that they quote other famous poets.

> *'Let me not to the marriage of true minds*
> *Admit impediments. Love is not love*
> *Which alters when it alteration finds,*
> *Or bends with the remover to remove:*
> *O no! it is an ever-fixed mark*
> *That looks on tempests and is never shaken;*
> *It is the star to every wandering bark,*
> *Whose worth's unknown, although his height be taken.*
> *Love's not Time's fool, though rosy lips and cheeks*
> *Within his bending sickle's compass come:*
> *Love alters not with his brief hours and weeks,*
> *But bears it out even to the edge of doom.*
> *If this be error and upon me proved,*
> *I never writ, nor no man ever loved.'*

"Shakespeare," she whispered. "Sonnet 116. It's one of my favorites."

"Has George ever recited poetry for you?"

"Heaven's no." She waved her hand dismissively. "I'm not even certain George knows any poetry. Well, I mean obviously he would have been educated in the verse as you were, but he seems to favor other types of entertainment."

"Were I to court you, I would recite such verses, though

I would have to insist you not relay my secret to anyone. A man has to keep up his reputation, you see, and a gaming hell owner who recites Shakespeare is unacceptable at best."

Her lips twitched in a smile. "Your secret is safe with me. That is, *if* you were courting me."

"Which I am not."

"Of course not." She was quiet for a moment. "But if you were, what else, besides poetry, how else would you woo me?"

"Riding in the park is nice, but I'd prefer someplace a little more intimate, more private."

Her eyebrows rose. "Is that so?"

"Indeed. For instance, people would be shocked and scandalized if I kissed you in the middle of Hyde Park, or say in the middle of a waltz at Lord Abernathy's estate."

"Oh my goodness." She leaned in a little closer, and it was all the encouragement he needed.

With one arm, he pulled her closer then dropped his mouth to hers. It was a kiss meant to show her what she could have outside of a marriage with George. A kiss meant to show her she was desirable just as she was, not some enhanced version of herself. But the instant his lips touched hers, he forgot all about his intentions.

Her lips were soft and pliant beneath his. With only a tiny amount of coaxing, he was able to open her mouth and explore inside. Her warm breath mingled with his.

God, she felt so good, tasted so sweet. He deepened the kiss and felt her fingers lace through his hair. Her tongue moved against his, fueling his arousal. Damnation, but he wanted her. Right here, right now on the floor of his billiard room. Or better yet, up against the billiards table.

He fought the urge to groan and forced himself to end the kiss.

Her eyes remained closed, and her breath came in shallow puffs. Then she opened her eyes and smiled at him. "I suspect your manner of courtship would be quite effective."

. . .

In the carriage back to her townhome Clarissa replayed the two kisses she'd received that evening. The one with George, she'd instigated, but then somehow had lost control of and it had been an utter disaster. A rather unpleasant disaster at that. There was nothing particularly wrong with George's kiss; his technique had been different than Justin's, but still a passionate kiss. And yet she'd felt nothing. Well, nothing save panic to end it quickly.

Contrast to the one she'd received from Justin, which had affected her in both body and soul, it seemed. Of course it hadn't hurt that he'd quoted her favorite poem. If she could only read one author and listen to one composer, it would be Shakespeare and Beethoven. They'd been her favorites since she'd been a girl. So to say she'd been ripe for the plucking, as it were, would be an understatement. She only wished she could contribute her entire reaction to Shakespeare. Unfortunately, she had begun to sink beneath Justin's spell long before he'd brought out the poetry. She did not think of herself as a vain woman, but his compliments had turned her head and warmed her to the very core. No man had ever said such things to her. And even if one had, she doubted she would have believed him. However, it was different with Justin. He had a way of looking at a woman is gaze seared into her, making her warm all over. If continued to find him so irritating, she would have a list of things for which she needed to apologize. And what was so grating about him? His handsomeness, decided. Yes, that was it, he was simply too handsome. ctically speaking no one needed to be *that* attractive. ll, and it wasn't so much that she was irritated with him it was the fact that he made her want things she had no ght to want. Namely, him. "Do you know how?" she asked.

His gaze darkened. "I know you believe I must have een raised in the forest with wolves, but try to remind ourself that I attended the same school as your brother. I can assure you I'm a rather accomplished dancer."

Clarissa swallowed. How was it he could be so unfazed by such a nasty question when mere glances of his sent her heart into acrobatics? "That's not what I meant to ask. I was merely surprised you'd be interested in dancing, that's all. But since you've so eloquently reminded me that you were raised properly, I should like to see you prove such a thing," she countered, hoping that he wouldn't notice her hands were shaking. Clarissa held out her dance card and allowed him to write down his name. Once he was done, she smiled slightly. "If you will excuse me, I believe I see my friend Ella over there." She turned and walked away. She did her best not to run to her friend.

"Did he just ask you to dance?" Ella asked once Clarissa reached her side.

"He did."

Ella grabbed her dance card to look at it. "A waltz too. Oh how positively scandalous. I think I might swoon."

"You will do no such thing."

that made her believe he could see right to her very soul. And that what he saw there entranced him. It was heady stuff, being wooed by Justin Rodale.

Why was her reaction so very different from one man's kiss to the other's? It truly made no sense. Since she had romantic feelings for George, had planned to be his wife for the majority of her adult life, shouldn't his kisses be the ones making her knees wobble? Shouldn't his kiss be the one that caused such delicious sensations to coil through her body, teasing at her breasts, and ending up at the apex of her thighs?

Yet, it was Justin's kiss that made her feel so alive, so full of lust and desire.

Chapter Six

Clarissa and Aunt Maureen stepped into the ballroom that glowed with gold and green fabrics and hundreds of candles.

It was lovely and the air smelled of spiced punch. The musicians had already begun playing and a handful of people scattered about the dance floor moving to the country dance.

Clarissa was nervous. She wasn't certain why. She'd been to countless balls. But tonight her insides jittered like she'd had too much champagne. Justin had been invited, she'd been told. Evidently when Vivian had seen that he be invited to a handful of functions a few months ago, people had grown accustomed to his presence. Of course it probably didn't hurt that Justin's half-brother was the Duke of Chanceworth. But other people being used to his presence did not make it easier for her.

She never felt uneasy around him per se, especially when they were alone, but it was the fact that they'd spent so much alone time together that concerned her. Would people be

able to tell? Would others be able to see shared? Her cheeks flamed in response.

She was a perfect lady, she reminded she knew how to behave like a perfect lady. would have been proud to know, despite C actions. Kissing not one but two different me

She took a deep breath. She loved balls. L and seeing her friends. She loved looking at al and she used to love gobbling up whatever gossip the night. Tonight she was less eager for that bit o she had so recently been the main dish.

Almost immediately one of Maureen's friends up and whisked Maureen away to go and hear about so's outrageous new hat. Clarissa stepped through cro people searching for Ella.

She wanted to see George. She wanted the reassu that things were still well between them since their Perhaps she should apologize for being so brazen. No, s wanted him to know she was available, that she would be good wife to him in every way. She searched the room for hi handsome face, but as she looked, he was not the man that caught her attention. Instead of George's golden good looks, she was struck by a tall man with the more olive complexion and eyes as dark as sin. She sucked in a breath. Her heart quivered and flipped and she tried her best to swallow the sensations so that they did not reveal themselves on her face.

Justin Rodale stood across the room. He nodded to her, allowing his gaze to take in the length of her. He took a step toward her, then came the rest of the way.

"Good evening," he said, but he never took his eyes off hers. "I would very much enjoy a dance."

Clarissa looked down and Justin had most certainly signed his name by a waltz. "He should know better."

"I suspect he knows precisely what he's doing," Ella said. "He is no stranger to Society. Wasn't he raised in the Duke of Chanceworth's home?"

"He was, but I know he was not treated as a son." She remembered hearing him saying such things when he'd come over as a young man. He had confided in Marcus, and she'd overheard their discussions.

Ella started to clap. "Oh, look at Mr. Rodale now, he is positively charming Lady Primrose right out of her knickers."

"Ella, honestly," Clarissa said. But she followed her friend's gaze across the ballroom and there was Justin talking to Lady Primrose, her plump figure bobbed as she laughed at something he said. She placed her fan on his forearm, he said something, and then she laughed again.

"What is he doing?" Clarissa asked.

"Talking to her. Blending in quite well, I might add," Ella said.

"What do we have here, Lady Ella and Lady Clarissa," a woman said as she walked up. "What are you two gossiping about?"

Clarissa eyed the woman. Lady Benchly was a notorious gossip and had a reputation for being rather mean-spirited as well. Clarissa had never cared for her.

"Lady Benchly," Clarissa and Ella said in unison.

"No gossip here," Ella said.

Lady Benchly smiled. "I suppose that is for the best. Clarissa here certainly knows how damaging gossip can be, don't you dear?"

"I don't believe I do," Clarissa said, deliberately being obtuse.

"Oh, don't be daft girl, certainly you must know that tongues are wagging about a clandestine meeting between you and the owner of that gambling establishment. Positively scandalous. And to think he's been invited here, among us." Lady Benchly clicked her tongue and shook her head.

"I hadn't realized that coordinating with a family friend about a brother's return to London was scandalous. If so, I suppose I am rather guilty," Clarissa said with a smile. "Seems if I were planning a clandestine meeting, I would have been more discreet than speaking to a gentleman on the street. Then again perhaps it is only the people who have intimate knowledge of clandestine meetings who imagine the worst. I admit to being naïve about such matters."

Lady Benchly pursed her lips. "I don't know what you're insinuating, Lady Clarissa, but I do not appreciate your attitude."

"You know I hadn't realized that particular shade of yellow had returned to fashion, Lady Benchly," Ella said. "But you always have been above reproach," she said brightly.

Lady Benchly's expression pinched her features. "Good evening to you ladies," she said, then strolled away.

"Ella, you shouldn't have insulted her like that."

"She deserved it." Ella crossed her arms over her chest. "She was positively horrible to you. And she does look really ugly in that color."

"That color would be ugly on anyone." Clarissa said. Just then George and Ella's brother, Victor, stepped over to them.

"I believe I'd like some lemonade. Refreshment table?"

"Sounds delightful," Ella said. "Of course, anything would be delightful after conversing with that old bag."

"Ella!"

"It's true." She smiled. "You know you can't even argue with me on that."

"Good evening ladies," George said. "Clarissa, would you dance with me?"

She handed him her dance card. "Of course."

He shook his head. "No, right now, this dance."

"Yes, certainly."

Ella frowned, but Clarissa left her standing there with her brother. The music began and Clarissa realized it was a quadrille, not one of her favorites because you had to keep switching partners, but it was lively. She began standing across from George, moved forward, they touched hands, she tried to think of something to say, something clever or engaging, but nothing came to mind.

"Clarissa, you look quite lovely this evening," George said.

"Thank you," she said and then was whisked off to another partner, and another. She wanted to ask George about Franny, demand he tell her the truth about his intentions, but she didn't dare do such a thing. She wasn't even supposed to know about the wager.

"Are you having a pleasant evening?" he asked again once they were back together.

"Indeed and yourself?" Oh these pleasantries were enough to drive her to madness. She wanted to have a real conversation with him, talk about something that mattered. But even if she could do such a thing, this particular dance was not conducive to such a discussion.

"Who was that gentleman you were speaking to earlier?" George asked.

Clarissa ignored the heat that surged through her. "That

was Mr. Rodale. He is a dear friend of the family."

"I see."

"What is it, George, do you have something to say about Mr. Rodale?"

He eyed her for a moment, then nodded slightly. "I am concerned for your welfare. I'd hate to see a man such as he tarnish your impeccable reputation."

The words shocked her, so much so that she nearly missed the fact that the music had ended and their dance was over. "Thank you for your concern. I can assure you that my reputation is quite all right." She realized with alarming clarity that she was angry with George. He was the one who had lied to her, who had treated their relationship, or whatever it was, so casually. And yet he had the nerve to feign concern. The fact that the concern was warranted did not escape her mind. Her reputation should be in tatters now as many times as she'd been alone with Justin, kissed Justin.

George escorted Clarissa back to Ella, then he bent over Clarissa's hand and walked away.

"What was that?" Ella asked.

"I believe George and I just had our first fight, only he doesn't know it and I didn't say anything."

"I'm not certain I followed that. Still want something to drink?"

"Most definitely." Perhaps she should have had Justin teach her how to sip some scotch. She could use something a little strong at the moment.

They reached the refreshment table and instead of selecting lemonade, which Clarissa had intended, she chose a glass of champagne. The bubbles teased her lips as she took a hearty sip.

Ella eyed her, surprise etched in her features. "Do you want to talk about it?"

"Not particularly." Clarissa scanned the room, the couples twirling around the middle of the ballroom, and then she spotted George. He stood over near the French doors that led to the balcony and he was obviously speaking with someone, but his body blocked the person from Clarissa's view. And then George shifted, held his arm out and Franny Cooper took it and then he escorted her outside. "Look at that." She nodded with her head.

Ella followed Clarissa's gaze to the couple as they left the ballroom. "A dance with you, a walk with her." Ella sighed. "He's certainly keeping up appearances as far as not letting on to which one of you he's going to pick."

Clarissa considered that a moment, wondered if right now he was kissing Franny in the gardens and if Franny would enjoy it more than Clarissa had. If only Rebecca were still alive to give her guidance. What if she didn't want to marry George, then what? It wasn't as if there were other prospects. She'd set her sights on George so early on, after the incident with Christopher, that she hadn't really encouraged any other would-be suitors.

Ella stilled, then nudged Clarissa in the ribs. "Listen," she whispered.

Clarissa's hand gripped her champagne glass and she focused on the people behind them.

"Well, that is not what I heard about him," one woman said. "No, I had heard that Mr. Rodale blackmailed someone to invite him to this very ball. Can you imagine?"

"It is not as if he'd have to resort to such extreme measures," another woman said. "His brother is a duke, for heaven's sake. Certainly if the man wanted to be a part of polite society, his brother could garner him invites."

"Lois, you always do give everyone the benefit of the doubt. That man is a bastard and he has no place in this ballroom with the rest of us," the first woman said. "I don't care if his father was a duke and his mother was nearly French royalty, it doesn't make it right."

Clarissa grit her teeth, feeling quite indignant on his behalf. Yes, she'd thought those very things about him, but she'd never say them in public. And now that she'd actually heard them out of someone's mouth, she could see how truly ugly the sentiment was.

"It is not his fault, the choices his parents made," the other woman argued.

Precisely. Clarissa tugged on Ella's sleeve. "I don't need to hear any more of that," she said once they were out of earshot. She didn't want a reason to feel defensive for him. It wasn't as if she could actually say anything on his behalf. That would really start the gossip flying.

"Do you know who his mother was?" Ella asked. "Do you believe she was a French princess or some such thing?"

"No, of course not." But the truth was Clarissa had no idea who his mother was. Other than knowing she was French, Clarissa had never given it a single thought.

Until now.

• • •

It was not difficult for Justin to locate Clarissa when it was time for their dance. His eyes had followed her all evening. He'd known where she'd been, to whom she'd spoken with, and which fellows brought her to dance. He'd seen her dance with George and then seen the man take Miss Cooper outside for a walk. Clarissa had not been pleased.

For most of the evening she stood next to her friend Ella. As he walked up to the two of them, Ella's eyes widened.

"I believe this is our dance, Chrissy," he said.

He brought Ella's gloved hand to his lips and nodded. "Lady Ella, a pleasure as usual."

She giggled. "Mr. Rodale. You two are going to miss your dance, go."

Once Clarissa and Justin were on the dance floor, she blurted out, "I am quite sorry for my rudeness."

"When?" he asked.

Her cheeks pinkened. "Yes, well I realize I have been ill mannered when it comes to you on more than one occasion." She looked up at him. "It does seem that you have a tendency to bring that out in me, being around you makes me forget my manners and I'm far more likely to speak my mind. My apologies."

He nodded. "It is a strange thing to apologize for, would you not agree? What if I prefer you speak your mind? Prefer that you're honest? Prefer you to simply be yourself?"

She looked up at him a moment and he was struck by how perfectly beautiful she was, with her sparkling blue eyes and lips that he knew were far softer and more pliable than he had a right to know.

"Do you prefer that from everyone?" she asked.

"I'm not speaking of anyone but you, but I suppose yes, I think people should be honest." His eyes met hers. "And I do know other things about you. You need not pretend about anything around me."

She nodded. "You have done quite well tonight."

"What does that mean?" he asked. She was much shorter than him; he couldn't help noticing, so very feminine. He rather enjoyed having her in his arms in the midst of the people around them, having an acceptable excuse to put his hands at the curve of her waist, be close enough to catch the lovely lemon scent of her hair.

"Merely that you do very well blending in with everyone here."

Blending because he didn't belong—is what she meant? Clarissa didn't mean it poorly. It was the way she'd been raised, the way they'd all been raised—these people surrounding him tonight. How could she apologize in one breath and in the next insult him again? Then he realized she didn't mean it as an insult. More than likely she thought she paid him a compliment. Still her words stung.

He knew he didn't belong here. He'd known that his entire life. And some people felt the need to remind him of that. But he also knew that regardless of what people thought of him, he'd been invited and he'd come and he would do his damnedest to blend in as much as possible because that made people uncomfortable.

That didn't really explain why he was truly there. He did feel indebted to the Kincaid family since they'd always been so welcoming of him. But he knew his recent jaunt into Society had more to do with a certain Kincaid than out of gratitude to the entire brood.

"Chrissy, you look beautiful tonight," he said, knowing fully that the compliment would make her uncomfortable.

"Why do you call me that?" she asked.

She looked up at him and the startling shade of blue in

her eyes met his. "Because it irritates you. And when you're irritated, you get feisty. I like it when you're feisty, when I can see the fire burn behind your eyes. It makes you more interesting."

She took a deep breath and swallowed, then schooled her features so that she was once again pretty Clarissa Kincaid, not his spirited Chrissy.

"I imagine you know all manner of secrets about many of the families in this room," she said. She looked around at the couples dancing near them. "I suspect you also make many of them quite nervous simply by being here."

Justin glanced around. "You are right on both accounts. You are obviously uneasy about dancing with me."

"What makes you say that?"

"You insist on talking."

"It is what we're supposed to do whilst we dance," she said. "Why, what do you think dancing is about?"

"Holding a beautiful woman close in your arms. The music, the swell of the strings, the way our bodies move as one. The heated pink stain in your cheeks, the catch of your breath, the way your back feels against my hand. The fact that in just the right angles I get a tantalizing view down your bodice."

Her mouth had fallen open, but she came to her senses and closed it.

"*That* is what dancing is about to me."

"Well," she said as she tilted her chin up, "perhaps that is what it is to some. But for proper society, it is about witty conversation."

"We can talk if it will put you more at ease."

She grinned, satisfied with his acquiesce. "Will you tell

me some of them?"

"Some of what?" he asked.

"The secrets? The gambling details?" she asked.

"Chrissy, shame on you," he said with a grin of his own. "I am discreet, you know that. It is a hallmark of my business. Rodale's wouldn't be nearly as popular a gaming hell if people thought their secrets were being bandied about at the balls." He swirled her around the dance floor, noting that she felt rather perfect in his arms. It had been years since he'd danced. He'd forgotten that, at times, it could be enjoyable.

"You are no fun at all," she said.

He considered her for a moment, then nodded. "Very well, I offer a deal instead," he said. "You provide me with some tidbit of gossip you know and I will give you a piece of information in return. Tit for tat, if you will."

Clarissa looked up at him, her blue eyes sparkling. She nodded slowly. "I suppose I could do that. Ella's mother does love her gossip so I hear my fair share of it."

"Ah, well then our deal is off," he said.

Her expression fell into disappointment. "Whatever for?"

"How can I trust you not to share these bits of gossip with her? Rodale's would be ruined if word got out that I had divulged private information with you," he said.

"But *I* am not the gossip," she said. She bit at her lip. "What if I promise not to? You can trust me."

He raised one brow. "Can I?"

She sucked in a breath, but never took her eyes off him. "Yes," she said quietly. "Of course you can."

"Excellent. You go first. Tell me about that woman," he said nodding to the woman dancing next to them. She was probably in her fourth decade and age was beginning to show in her features, though she still worked hard to make herself look attractive. The man she danced with was clearly younger than her, but seemed pleased to have the lady in his arms.

Clarissa looked over and nodded briefly. "That is Lady Bandy," she said quietly. "She has been a widow for years. It is said she takes a new lover at the start of every Season."

Justin smiled. "Now then. I could tell you that Lord Bleacher has a significant problem with hazard."

Clarissa's eyes widened. "What is it?"

"He has virtually no luck at all. He owes a tremendous amount of money, but he has more than that in his coffers, so I suspect no one overly cares." He looked around again. "The group of women standing over there near the refreshment table, tell me about the one in the green dress."

She glanced over, then pinched her features. "That is Mildred Cutter and *she* refuses to wear corsets." Clarissa shook her head as if that was a truly vile offense.

Justin chuckled. "Shocking," he said.

"Do not mock, it is not as if she does not need one."

He looked back over at the woman.

"Stop it, now you're staring. Tell me about Viscount Sanders, I've heard he has a terrible gambling problem," she said.

He sighed. "Yes, it is significant. Poor fellow, he has terrible instincts, plays all the wrong people. I am working with him and he owes me a lot of money. Last week I sent him away. I will no longer allow him to play with money he does not have."

She shook her head almost in disbelief, then a slight furrowing of her brow. "That was very kind of you."

Justin nearly missed a step. The way she was looking at

him as if he'd done something amazing when he'd only done the responsible thing, save his business from more losses.

"I don't suppose it will prevent him from going to another establishment," she said.

"No, and men enjoy playing with him because they know they'll win. If he's not careful, he'll lose his house. He's already had to dismiss most of his servants."

"That's terrible. Explains why his wife was so quiet at the card party the other day," Clarissa said.

The song ended and he stopped their dancing. He took her arm to lead her back to Ella. "How was your dance with George?"

She stopped abruptly and looked up at him. "It was as enjoyable as that particular dance can be. It's not one of my favorites."

His brows rose. "Thank you for being honest with me."

"I suppose you saw him leave with Miss Cooper as well. Have they returned?"

"She returned sometime during our dance. I have not seen Wilbanks," he said.

"You notice everything, don't you?"

"I have to at Rodale's so it carries over to wherever I am." He'd been like that as a boy, though. Roe's mother had always told him it was a good trait and it would serve him well in life.

"Thank you for a lovely dance," she said.

"You're welcome. I hope to see you soon." He bowed to her and walked away. He rolled his eyes. She had taken him off guard, though, with the moony way she'd looked at him, the awe in her voice. He was not some hero to be applauded. He was nothing more than a businessman. A bastard.

Chapter Seven

After he'd left the ball, Justin returned to Rodale's. The gaming floor was still a little quiet, but people were beginning to arrive. He nodded to the few men gathered at a table playing baccarat, then made his way up the stairs to the offices. He had no sooner entered the room when Clipps cleared his throat.

"I have found out some information on that bloke you wanted me to look into."

Justin sat and eyed his friend. "Spill it, man."

"He frequents Rafferty's."

So Justin's instinct had been correct. George had told Clarissa his debts were at Rodale's because it was the most respectable hell. Rafferty's was another gaming hell, perhaps equally as popular as Rodale's, but in a very different part of town, down on the docks of the Thames. "And you're certain?"

"Yes, I followed him myself. On two separate evenings he left here and went there. I spoke with a handful of workers there that knew him by name and said he came several nights a week. He has a penchant for fighting."

"Boxing? Well, that explains why he isn't playing here more often, if that's his preference for wagering. Does he bet only or does he fight?"

"Oh, he fights. Inside the ring and out, evidently he has quite the temper. He's quite good though, I'm told, doesn't owe them money either," Clipps said.

A temper. So the man liked plenty of women and he had a penchant for hitting things. Not a good combination, and most certainly not a good choice for Clarissa. Justin would never forgive himself it he stood by and allowed her to marry the man and then found out he hit her. He'd kill George Wilbanks himself if that happened. "Thank you, Clipps." Frequenting Rafferty's alone would have been enough to prove Wilbanks wasn't the right man for her. That club had dedicated itself to serving the needs of those who preferred more risky methods of entertainment. "Did he accompany anyone there or did he go alone?" Justin asked.

"Alone, but it did not take him long to find companionship for the evening."

This was the man that Clarissa said she intended to marry and he'd already lied to her about having debts. But why lie about money owed? Even if the man did prefer a gaming hell on the docks inhabited by opium addicts and high stake games.

Justin needed additional information. She deserved more than a man who would lie to her, let alone one would be unfaithful and strike her in anger.

"What do you want me to do now?" Clipps asked.

"Nothing. I'll look into matters further." He nodded to

the ledger books on Clipps's desk.

"How is he doing here?"

"Winning. When he plays. He doesn't always play. He has a drink, makes a few wagers, and then slips out."

Justin made a note to check the wager book before he left to see where Clarissa stood that day. If the bets were favoring her, then he would need to move quickly to dissuade her from her plan.

It sounded as if George Wilbanks did not prefer Rodale's at all; he merely used it as a cover for him to enjoy Rafferty's. Before Justin said anything to Clarissa, he needed to be certain. He would go there himself and see what Wilbanks was up to.

But first he wanted to see Clarissa again, try to talk some sense into her. He'd practically grown up in the Kincaid townhome and he still remembered all the ways to sneak in and out, methods he and Marcus had perfected as boys. He just hoped Clarissa's bedchamber was still in the same spot.

• • •

Clarissa rolled over again, situating herself amidst the pillows and held the book up to see it in the glow from the lantern. She hated feeling so confused. Before Justin had come back into her life, she'd never once questioned whether or not George was the man for her. Rebecca had suggested him and Clarissa had spent the majority of her adult life pursuing that relationship.

And she knew she should trust Rebecca'a advice. Clarissa had not done well at all when she'd selected her first suitor. Christopher had broken her heart and nearly stolen all of her jewelry she had from her mother. He'd then moved on from her to another heiress and then another and finally had been shunned from Society. Last she heard he was living somewhere in Scotland. She had learned then that her choices weren't always the best and it was better for her to trust someone else's guidance, namely her sister-in-law's.

Then Rebecca had died and left Clarissa with one last piece of advice—*that's the type of man you should marry.* Since Rebecca was no longer around to give her other suggestions of the "type" Clarissa had simply stuck with George. Until Justin and his shocking words and delicious kisses and his reciting of Shakespeare, she'd been content to wait for George to propose. Now it seemed she didn't have the luxury of waiting—she had competition.

She'd watched Franny Cooper tonight. The woman was so comfortable with men, easy with them, flirting appeared effortless and it never seemed she reserved those sweet smiles for only the wealthy handsome men; she treated all of them the same. Even the old, balding men, she would pat them on the arm with her fan and release one of her twittering laughs. Everyone liked her, men and women, old and young. She, it seemed, was the perfect lady.

Somehow Clarissa had fallen short yet again, and she hadn't a clue how to fix it or how to change herself. She'd tried to seek out Justin to teach her to be more worldly, but that had only seemed to make her want him more than she already had.

There was a creak outside her door and she wondered if Aunt Maureen had roused for something, a drink perhaps. Clarissa sat up in bed, listening intently and then her door opened.

It was on her tongue to ask if Maureen felt all right, but then Clarissa realized who had entered her room.

"Justin? What the devil are you doing here?" She pulled the coverlet up her chest to try to cover herself. Her nightrail was not particularly revealing, but was certainly more flimsy than a day dress.

"I wanted to see you," he said with a slight shrug of his shoulders. "Do you want me to leave?"

She couldn't make herself say the word, so she merely shook her head. "How did you get in here?"

He grinned. "Not much has changed here."

"I suppose that is true." Her eyes traveled around her room and she caught sight of her dressing gown draped across her vanity chair. "Could you hand me that?" She pointed to it.

He retrieved it and brought it to her, then turned away from her without her having to ask. He was a bit of a contradiction at times. Seducing her with sinful kisses one day and behaving the gentleman the next. It was enough to make a girl's head spin.

She crawled out of bed and in doing so she knocked her book to the floor. While he bent to pick it up, she pulled on her dressing gown.

"Shakespeare," he said as he turned to face her.

"Yes, well, you reminded me that I had not read him in a while." It wasn't really the truth. This particular volume of his sonnets stayed next to her bed all the time, she read it almost daily. But she didn't want Justin to know how much his wooing charade had affected her.

He came to stand in front of her. He leaned close, then around her to place the book on the bed behind her. He was so close she had a difficult time breathing, he smelled so good too, all masculine and clean and Justin. She resisted the urge to inhale deeply.

"What was it you wanted to see me about?"

He leaned in and put his nose beside her left ear and slowly inhaled. "You smell nice," he said as if he'd read her mind.

Chills scattered all over Clarissa's body and she felt her breasts tighten. *Oh my*. Had he come here to seduce her? Her pulse sped up as did her breathing. She wasn't certain that if that was in fact his intention she had the strength to tell him no. She knew she didn't want to.

He leaned even closer and she felt his warm breath on her neck. She closed her eyes just as he took her earlobe in his mouth and suckled it.

Desire coiled so quickly through her body, she feared she would melt into the plush rug beneath her feet. She turned her head ever so slightly and he grabbed her fiercely and pressed his lips to hers. His body molded against hers pressing her already sensitive breasts to his chest.

Kissing in nothing more than her night clothes was a different experience than doing so while fully clothed. At the moment she had no buffer between her breasts and his body other than the sheer fabric of her dressing gown and nightrail. As he kissed her, he pressed against her and with each slight movement, the fabric brushed against her aching nipples until she thought she'd go mad from it.

He pushed her back onto her bed and fell over her, all the while trailing searing kisses over her neck, collarbone and ears.

Oh, how she wanted him. Wanted whatever pleasure he could give her. She knew it was wrong. She knew it was improper, immoral even. But she also knew it was completely irresistible.

His lips met hers and his tongue tantalized her. Teasing, licking, stroking until she thought she would go mad. Their tongues stroked and played and shivers cascaded over her like delicious waterfalls of pleasure.

She felt his arousal push into her belly and she instinctively pushed against him.

His hand slid up her abdomen and cupped her right breast. Her back arched, and she felt her nipples harden. Good heavens, she'd never felt such sensations. He kneaded the sensitive flesh and the tingles between her legs intensified.

With a movement full of impatience, he slipped his hand beneath her dressing gown and stroked her aching nipple through the soft fabric of her nigthrail. His mouth left hers and blazed a trail to her ear, then down her throat and finally took the place of his hand. He kissed her breast through the fabric and she wanted to ask him to tear it off her, to touch her flesh, but she kept her mouth shut.

She bucked against him, wanting more, wanting release, wanting him.

"Oh, Justin."

"I know what you want, love," he said.

He dipped the fabric down, looked at her exposed breast for several breaths and then lowered his mouth to her. She plunged her fingers into his hair and did her best to not cry out so delicious were the pleasures he created.

"I want you," she whispered, unable to keep the sentiment to herself any longer.

He swore, then rolled off her. He came to his feet and stepped away from her, his hands clenched at his sides. "Chrissy, I'm sorry. I didn't mean…" He shook his head.

She covered herself back up and slowly came to her feet. "What's the matter?"

"I can't do this. Not with you." Then he turned and slipped out the door.

Not with her? What did that mean? What was the matter with her? He had told her on more than occasion he found her beautiful. So why not her?

More importantly why did she need him to want her? He was certainly not a suitor and they were not going to marry, so why did it matter? The easy answer was because it felt good. She was obviously attracted to him and his touch did amazing things to her body.

She'd never before been touched or kissed in such a way, and though it might be horribly unladylike, she loved it, loved the desire coursing thick through her blood. It wasn't merely the sensations, though, because deep down she knew those embraces wouldn't be the same with just anyone.

It terrified her to examine the situation closer to discover the truth. She was playing a dangerous game, and if she kept at it, she knew she would lose.

• • •

What the hell had he been thinking? Justin chose to send his rig on the way and walk home, hoping the cool night air would chill away his residual desire. He'd almost taken her. She would have allowed him to, but he could not ask that of her. He'd marry her, but damned if that would ruin her life as she imagined it. Her late sister-in-law, Rebecca, had never cared for him. He'd known that when he was younger. She'd found him sullen, and though she'd never said anything, he always felt she thought his birth made him unfit to be so friendly with their family.

He needed to take more care where Chrissy was concerned. He could not afford to hurt her. He'd only intended to speak with her about George, tell her the truth about his behavior. Certainly she wouldn't want to marry a man who enjoyed physically pounding on people. But she could only make that decision if he actually gave her the information instead of pawing at her like some randy schoolboy. Next time he saw her, he'd tell her the truth about George.

• • •

After much deliberation and a letter from Vivian again detailing how beneficial his assistance could be, Justin had agreed to court Miss Riverton. So it was that he found himself attending yet another ball only two days after the last one. This was becoming a disturbing pattern. It has also been the night he'd gone to see Chrissy and he knew he needed to talk to her, give her some explanation, but what would he say? He couldn't tell her the truth.

That he wanted her for himself.

In the meantime, he'd keep his focus on Miss Riverton and hope that when it came time to speak to Clarissa, he found the right words. They were dancing now, he and Betsy, and she was a pleasant girl, if not a little overly verbose.

Justin could feel Clarissa's eyes on him even as he twirled Miss Riverton around the ballroom floor. She was a sweet girl, though she chattered incessantly about horses. A fine species they were, and quite necessary for transportation, but he'd never had a particular affinity for the creatures. Perhaps her fascination with them was why other men had not been interested in courting her. Still, he had agreed to stand in as a suitor for her to get the attention of perhaps some other men.

"Miss Riverton," he said.

She started at the sound of his voice. "I'm sorry I was going on again." She gave him a weak smile. "I suppose I blather on when I get nervous."

"First, you shouldn't be nervous. I am merely a man. Also, one thing you should take note of with most men, they like to talk about themselves," he said. "Do not change who you are for any man, the lot of them aren't worth it, but perhaps take a breath every now and again to allow the man to get a word in."

That earned him a bigger smile. "I suspect that is quite excellent advice, Mr. Rodale. Thank you. Would you like to talk about yourself?"

"No, my life is vastly boring," he said, giving her a wink.

She laughed.

There was nothing wrong with Miss Riverton, he decided. She only needed the right man to take notice.

Appearing to court one of the Ton's darlings was raising some eyebrows and ruffling some feathers. Judging by the way a certain woman was looking in his direction, some of those feathers belonged to Clarissa Kincaid.

After their dance, Justin escorted Betsy to the refreshment table and handed her a glass of lemonade. She smiled coyly and then he returned her to her mother who eyed him suspiciously. The girl could do worse than him. Yes, he was a bastard, but he had more money than most of the families in here. He wanted to remind her that she was the one who had sought Vivian's assistance with her daughter, but he nodded to the woman and walked off.

Marcus walked over to Justin. "I see that my beloved wife has not retired as she suggested she might. When did she convince you to take on this little task?"

Justin smiled. "The other night at dinner. And then again in a letter. She's quite persuasive. And good at what she does."

"Yes, she is," Marcus said without an ounce of irritation. "On both accounts. In truth, I'm glad people still seek her out. She risked everything revealing her past, and it's nice that some people don't seem bothered by it."

"You weren't," Justin said.

Marcus shook his head. "No. We've all done things we aren't proud of. Women are no different."

Justin glanced at the room around them.

"What's wrong with the chit?" Marcus asked.

"Who?"

"The Riverton girl," Marcus said.

"Nothing. Well, she favors horses a little too much, can't seem to stop talking about them. But she's pleasant enough and obviously intelligent," Justin said.

"There you go. Smart women intimidate the lot of them." Marcus motioned to the crowd in front of them.

He was likely right. Plenty of men found a woman with opinions to be unconventional and mouthy. He'd found, though, that he actually preferred a woman with a mind of her own.

A specific woman.

Briefly he considered bringing his concerns about

George to Marcus's attention, but he knew if he did that Chrissy might not forgive him.

• • •

Clarissa had been watching Justin all evening. Dancing with Betsy Riverton, making her laugh, getting refreshment for her, behaving suspiciously as if he were courting the girl. But certainly that couldn't be the truth. His attentions to the girl stung, Clarissa couldn't deny that, especially in light of what had transpired between the two of them night before last.

She'd gone through scenarios in her mind again and again, trying to figure out how to ask him about what he'd meant.

Not with you.

There was nothing really to say. He didn't want her, had obviously been kissing her before that to, what, entertain himself? She didn't know. Ultimately she had decided that perhaps it was best to not mention the night in her bedchamber. Yet, she couldn't make herself walk away from him. And seeing him dote on Betsy made that even more difficult.

Clarissa came up behind Justin and whispered, "Ask to take me on a walk." Before he could turn around to face her, she walked off and met Aunt Maureen and Ella where they stood by the potted ferns. They were discussing the weather.

"It has been unusually warm for this time of year," Ella said.

Justin walked up casually and smiled, greeting each of them. "Lady Clarissa, may I escort you on a walk?"

She gave him a smile. "Indeed. Thank you for asking."

"I shall have her back in a few moments," he added for

Maureen's sake. He took her arm and they walked out onto the balcony.

The night was chilly, but not so cold she'd require her cloak, but she was thankful this particular ball gown had sleeves that went to her elbows and her gloves covered the rest of her arms. His warmth surrounded her too, and she wanted to lean into him, but knew better of it.

They went to sit on a bench. The balcony was well lit and they were close enough to the opened French doors from the ballroom that they could still hear the music. Why not me, she wanted to ask, but didn't, afraid of what his answer might be.

"I know what you're doing," she said instead.

"I beg your pardon?"

"With Betsy, you are trying to stir up trouble by appearing to court a lady." She hoped she was right and that it wasn't that he found Betsy Riverton irresistible. Not that she should care what he thought of other women, but certainly there were better choices out there. She couldn't imagine cheerful Betsy being the recipient of one of his heated gazes or even still, one of his passionate kisses. Her face warmed.

He chuckled and she worried for a moment that he had read her thoughts. "Is that what I'm doing?"

"Of course, I am no fool."

"You know I could never marry a woman from proper society," he said.

His words sliced through her. She knew it was the truth, knew *she* could never marry him, yet hearing him admit it still bothered her. "No, of course not, you're merely trying to raise some eyebrows."

"Now, why would I want to stir up trouble?"

Good heavens but he looked so very dashing this evening. Every time the breeze blew by, she'd catch a whiff of his soap and shaving lotion. Things were going well between them. It had always been easy to be around Justin, there was no reason to think that one night would alter that. "Because you want to make them nervous. You want to worry them."

He leaned over to her, nudged her a little with his body, then sat back straighter. "You believe me to be that transparent? Think you have it all figured out."

She swallowed hard. "No, of course not," she said hurriedly. "I only meant that I can certainly understand such a motive. People can be unkind." And she meant that. If this town had treated her as poorly as they had him, she would want to turn them up on their ear.

"Indeed. So then if I were courting some woman to cause trouble, as you say, then you would approve of such actions?"

"Of the practice in general, yes, but I know Betsy and unfortunately you have selected the wrong girl."

"I have?" He smiled at her, his eyes dropping to her lips. "I suppose you have another suggestion?"

Her heartbeat sped. Maybe he did still want her, despite what he'd said in her bedchamber. "I do. The way I see it, if you court any of these women, they will fall for you, be utterly seduced and entranced by your wicked good looks, and ultimately you will break their hearts."

"Tragic," he said.

"Precisely. None of them know you well enough to resist falling for you."

"Because of my wicked good looks."

She tried not to smile with him, but failed. "I am being quite serious."

"My apologies, please continue." He gave her a slight bow.

"What you should be doing is courting me." She looked up at him.

Both of his eyebrows rose, then a smiled settled on his lips. "I'll give you this, Chrissy, you never cease to surprise me. I did not see that coming."

Frankly, it surprised her too that she'd thought it, let alone said it aloud. But she couldn't let him know that so she quickly thought of an explanation. "It makes perfect sense. You get to do what you want, irritate the entitled, but you need not worry about breaking my heart."

"Because you are not seduced by my wicked good looks."

"Precisely." *Lie, lie, lie.* His wicked good looks were the problem entirely. Well, perhaps not entirely, there was the matter of those intoxicating kisses…

"Your logic is intriguing, I shall grant you that."

"Do you agree?"

"I'll consider your proposal."

Not with you. She schooled her features to ensure her disappointment wouldn't show.

"I do have a question, though," he said. "Won't my courting you cause problems between you and George?"

This is what she got for speaking before clearly thinking something through. This was what Rebecca had always warned her about, her impetuous nature. She'd seen Justin dancing with Betsy and had wanted to speak to him and then out popped that suggestion. But now that she considered it, perhaps a feigned courtship would be precisely what George needed to jump into action. And he certainly wasn't keeping himself all to her; he had Franny Cooper and who knew what other lady hanging on the line waiting for him.

"A little jealousy never hurt anyone."

He chuckled again. "Ah, Chrissy, I have missed you."

His words warmed her. Had he thought of her all these years? She had thought of him in passing, but had assumed that she'd never see him again. It had seemed a good thing at the time since Rebecca had thought him to be the wrong sort of boy to befriend Marcus.

"I do have a confession though," he said.

"Which is?"

He leaned close enough to her ear. "I'm not truly courting Miss Riverton."

"Yes, I know, that's what I was saying."

"No, you misunderstand." He sat straight again. "Vivian asked me to pay court to Miss Riverton."

She frowned. "Whatever for?"

"To draw the attention of other would-be suitors."

She opened her mouth to say something, then closed it. Her frown intensified. She was annoyed that her sister-in-law would ask such a thing of Justin. But in truth she had no reason to be irritated. Still, part of it felt like a betrayal.

"Did you know that Lord Volley makes wagers on his wife's dog breeding?" Justin asked.

She smiled relieved that he had changed the subject considering she'd just asked him to court her for no apparent reason. They had done well the other night when they'd spoken of similar matters. "I did not, but I do know that Lady Volley is so entranced with said dogs that supposedly she allows them in her bed, but not her husband. And I believe she has seven of those furry little creatures."

"Fascinating," he said.

"Most assuredly."

"What do you know of that woman over there?" He nodded toward the stately older woman standing at the edge of the ballroom doors.

"Oh, that is Lady Pringle, and I'm afraid I have no gossip about her. She is a pinnacle of propriety," Clarissa said.

"*That* is Lady Pringle?"

"You have heard of her? It would seem her reputation far reaches even what I would have thought. Then again, Rebecca used to call her the finest lady in all of London."

He grinned, a devilish grin that made Clarissa's toes curl. "It would seem that I am the one holding the gossip on her."

"No!" But his grin did not falter. "Truly?" she asked.

"Indeed. Your mistress of decorum over there is also a notorious gambler. She uses a false name and sends a proxy in her stead, but she places wagers on nearly everything under the sun."

"You are lying."

"Absolute truth." He put his hand over his heart as if making a pledge.

She narrowed her eyes at him. "If she uses a proxy and a fake name, how do you know it's her?"

"I make it my business to know about everyone who patronizes Rodale's. I did not know what she looked like, but my investigation turned up her real name." He gave Clarissa a look. "I should go over there and introduce myself."

"You cannot do that. You simply cannot introduce yourself, it isn't done."

"Yes, but I am a bastard. People would expect such things from me." He shrugged. "But I will leave her alone. I do not want to lose her patronage. She is one of the more interesting ones."

Chapter Eight

They stood in silence, looking out at the night sky. He hadn't denied anything she'd said about him courting Betsy Riverton. And she wasn't certain he'd taken her completely serious when she'd suggested he court her. She wasn't even certain where that had come from. It had seemed like the best suggestion, though. She wouldn't get hurt. This was Justin, he was a friend and nothing more.

Despite her obvious attraction to him, she shouldn't develop any certain feelings toward him. He was not the sort of man Rebecca would have chosen for her. Clarissa needed to keep that in mind. Especially since she'd just proposed a scenario that would require the two of them spend more time together.

He looked over, gave her a half smile. "I have discovered some information on George. You wanted me to tell you."

She grabbed a handful of her skirts, bunching the fabric, then thought better of it and smoothed it out again. "I can tell from your tone that you are not pleased with what you discovered."

He eyed her for a moment, then was quiet for several more before he finally spoke. "I shall make a bargain with you."

She nodded unsure of what he would ask of her.

"Cease your obsession with George Wilbanks."

Her breath caught. Was he suggesting that he wished to replace George in her mind, in her favor? As wrong as it might be, she knew there was a part of her that hoped so. "I am not obsessed. I am merely dedicated to the notion of marrying him. He would be a good husband for me."

"No," Justin shook his head, "a *viscount* would be a good match for you, but not him."

"I am not so certain."

"I can prove to you that he is the wrong sort of man for you."

His words rang with truth, and she knew she'd be inclined to believe him. But to do so would be to ignore the advice of the one person who had done her best to steer Clarissa in the right direction. "Precisely how can you do that?"

"I can take you to Rafferty's."

"I don't think I know what that means," she said.

"It's another gaming hell. One on the banks of the Thames, next to the docks," he said.

She gasped. "You can do no such thing. I would be ruined." Though obviously she was already ruined. Still, to go to such a place with him, without a chaperone, it would be a blow to her reputation from which she could never recover.

"We could go without anyone seeing you."

She considered his offer. She was curious, she couldn't deny that.

"Chrissy, it's important. You need to know the truth about this man before you agree to marry him."

He was quite serious and his demeanor made her nervous. Anticipation fluttered to life in her stomach. "When?"

"Tonight. Do you think you can sneak out of your house without your brother or aunt being the wiser?"

Her heart thundered at the idea of sneaking out again. She'd done so on a handful of occasions recently and the adventure never ceased to thrill her. That old familiar pull toward adventure was a temptation she'd had to fight her entire life. Rebecca had helped her with that when she'd been alive, but since her death, Clarissa had battled on her own. "I don't know."

"It's your choice. But I do know that you won't believe me, you won't believe the truth about your beloved George unless you see it with your own eyes," Justin said.

She realized with alarming clarity that this entire conversation had been about George. Somehow she'd been so lost in idea of an adventure that she'd forgotten what it was all about. He knew something about George that would change her mind about pursuing him for her husband. She supposed she should go into the marriage with her eyes open. "Very well, I accept your invitation. What time shall I be ready?"

. . .

Soon Clarissa would be with him, ensconced in a darkened carriage as they drove London to the dirtier part of town. She hadn't asked him anything about the night in her bedchamber, instead she'd jested with him, flirted. And then she'd asked him to court her, an obvious reaction to seeing him with another woman. Still he knew that Chrissy didn't know what she asked of him. He could easily pretend to be interested in another girl, but to pretend to court her, he couldn't do that and know he'd never have her. So he'd changed the subject.

Convincing her to come tonight had been easier than he'd first thought it would be. She obviously believed he was wrong about her beloved George, or at least she wanted to continue believing him to be this pinnacle of gentlemanliness that she held him to.

Justin had tried to be discreet and make inquires of the man, but he hadn't discovered much other than he preferred Rafferty's and had a penchant for boxing. Clipps following the man had been the only thing that had shed any light on the situation. Justin wondered if Clarissa knew her would-be groom enjoyed a good fight. Or that he chose prostitutes for his evening entertainment?

Once Clarissa saw the man she believed she wanted to marry on the docks at Rafferty's she might begin to see that George Wilbanks was the very wrong sort of man for her.

• • •

Clarissa checked once more behind her to ensure no one followed. The darkened stairwell that led to the servant's entrance in the back of the house was a perfect way to get in and out of the estate. She opened the door and was met with darkness. Justin, true to his word, appeared as if out of nowhere.

"Ready?" he asked.

She took a deep breath. "Yes." She was determined to prove Justin wrong. George was not the wrong man for her. He couldn't be the wrong man for her because if she didn't marry George, who else would pick her? If after all of these years of everyone expecting them to marry and then he picks someone else, then no one would want her. She was already nearly on the shelf, as it were. She was running out of time and had already run out of options. No, she couldn't explain his reluctance to marry her, but she knew there had to be a reason. A good reason too. So she'd agreed to this journey knowing full well if she got caught, there would be no explaining this one. It was worth the risk. George was worth the risk.

Justin grabbed her hand and pulled her into the darkness in front of them. She should probably feel more fear than she did, but this was no time to question such things. She was on a quest.

They reached the carriage and Justin helped her inside, then followed her and closed the door behind him. He sat across from her, a walking stick rested against the seat next to him. It was an opulent carriage, with plush upholstery and a soft leather finish. His height was even more noticeable in the small confines. His broad shoulders seemed to take up nearly the entire bench across from her and his gloved hand resting on the walking stick looked so big, masculine. That hand had been on her body. Her cheeks heated and she shifted in her seat.

They rumbled down the alleyway behind her family's townhome.

"So we're going to the docks, to a place called Rafferty's?" she asked.

"You had never heard of it, until I mentioned it?" he asked.

"No, of course not. It is not the sort of thing people would discuss in front of a lady." She pulled back the tiny curtain and peered out the window. London's darkened streets slowly passed by. "And this is where you say George goes?"

"Yes, several nights a week."

"What sort of establishment is this Rafferty's? I mean should I find it sinful that he goes to this place?"

"It's a gaming hell."

"Like yours?"

"*Not* like mine. We share some things. We both offer games with high stakes, as any gambling establishment would, but there are some significant differences. Mine, for instance, is not in a wretched, filthy and dangerous part of town."

"I'm certain that if this is true, if George goes to this place, then there is a logical explanation," she said. She crossed her arms over her chest and prayed she was right. She had not been inside of Rodale's that night she'd stood outside, but she'd seen enough to know that it was opulent, much like this carriage.

Justin had built a massive fortune, and likely had more money than her own family. Arguably George could find whatever he needed at Rodale's, which begged the question of why he would frequent a gaming establishment on the docks of the Thames where everyone, even genteel ladies, knew that opium was rampant and prostitution was readily available.

"What is it about George?" Justin asked. "Besides Rebecca's recommendation?"

"We've known each other a very long time. He's a gentleman. We are an excellent match."

"Yes, an excellent match," Justin said, then he fell silent for a long time. "You say all of that as if you've rehearsed it for a long while. Are Ella and I the only ones who thing George is the wrong choice for you?"

"My Aunt Maureen is not overly fond of him either, but she knows how I feel about him."

"And how is that, Clarissa, do you love him?"

"I believe that I could love him."

"That's not really the same thing, is it?"

"No, I don't suppose it is. But people marry all the time without love."

"A pity," he said.

What did he mean by that? That he intended to marry for love? Her insides knotted and her palms began to itch with perspiration. They fell quiet for several moments before she spoke again. "What did you mean the other night when you said my piano playing was passionate?"

"I can tell from how you move with the music that it's inside you, that you love it. It lights you up," he said. "You play effortlessly."

"Thank you," she said and realized she fully meant it. He'd given her a lovely compliment.

"Your passion is evident. I could see it on your face, the way your body moved, the way your fingers flew over the keys. I very much enjoyed watching you play."

"You're not supposed to watch me, you're supposed to listen, hear the music." Was what he said true? Was it so obvious to others that she felt the music inside of her as if the notes were an extension of her bones? She felt her cheeks heat with embarrassment. A lady was not supposed to be so transparent, let alone so brazen. Then again, when it came to Justin, she had long since past the point of what a lady was supposed to do. Not only that, but being the perfect lady, or at least behaving as one, had certainly not gotten her where she'd wanted to be.

"I did listen" His voice was pitched low and sent a shiver through her. "Mozart, correct?"

That surprised her. "Yes, that's right."

"It surprises you that I know that," he said. "You should remember, Clarissa, I was raised in a household much like your own. I am a bastard by birth, but only because my father was a liar and a cheater."

There was hardness to his words. He was angry and she couldn't fault him for that. He deserved to be angry with his father. He'd been furious with his father since she'd known Justin. It seemed he had not let go of his anger towards his father, but he had learned how to temper himself. The circumstances of his birth hadn't been his own fault. Still society deemed that those of illegitimate blood were not true aristocrats no matter who their father was. "And your mother, the woman who raised you, you said she was a music teacher?"

He inclined his head. "Yes, before she moved to England." Some of the tension left his shoulders. "She taught in Paris."

"Your brother, are you two close?"

"We are now. Haven't always been. Roe is doing the title much more justice than our father did, though he would never admit as much."

"He's a noted gambler," she said. Funny that he would criticize George when his own brother had such disregard for his position in society.

"He's a gifted card player."

"You can say it with more polite words, but it doesn't make the truth any less true. He's a gambler, just as George obviously is." Again silence surrounded them and Clarissa was left wondering what they'd see when their journey ended. The lights of London shone outside of her window. They were getting close.

"You are correct, of course. But I think you'll see soon the full truth about George, not merely the penchant for wagering."

"Perhaps. What is it about placing wagers that is so very thrilling for me?" she asked.

"I gambled some in school. Thought it wasn't much of a gamble because I rarely lost. It's how I raised the money to start Rodale's. So I don't have much desire to bet and gamble, as it were. Though I do know something about you I'd wager."

"Indeed, and what would that be?"

"You would be a most passionate lover. I suspect no one else has recognized that in you. And I knew it, saw it in you even before we ever kissed."

"You are scandalous." But his words heated over her as if he'd reached across the carriage and touched her. Here in this darkened carriage where no one could see and yet he'd said things about the music and her playing as if he'd seen her, the real her, in a way that no one ever had.

"Perhaps. But no one can play the piano like that and not be a passionate person. It burns inside you, Clarissa, you merely need the right man to free it from its binds," he said.

"And I suppose you believe yourself to be that man."

She said the words before she thought them through. He was also the man who had walked out on her the other night.

Not with you.

"I could be," he said, his voice low and nearly a whisper.

She tried to say something, anything that would keep her from asking him why he'd left her, asking him why it couldn't be her. She knew why. At least she knew all the logical reasons. They were from different stations in life. He obviously believed in love matches, he'd said as much one time. If he had tender feelings toward her, he would have made that known.

"Come here." He didn't allow her time to argue with him. He pulled her across the carriage and onto the seat next to him—well, in truth she was part on the seat and part on him.

"Trust me," he whispered. And then he kissed her.

His lips were warm and gentle, and she tried to be unmoved by them, tried to ignore the desire coiling through them. But his kiss proved to be her complete undoing. She melted into him. His lips coaxed and she relented, opening to him. His tongue slid into her mouth a warm and shocking intrusion that sent shivers skittering across her flesh.

His hand cupped her face, pulling her closer to him and he deepened the kiss. Boldly, she moved her tongue against his and he groaned in response. Lust poured through her body, threatening to shut off every coherent thought, yet still she did not push him away. Finally he ended the kiss, but he only moved back from her enough so that she could see his face.

"Your kisses are intoxicating," he said. "I was right in my estimation of you."

"About the passion?" she asked dumbly.

"Yes. Chrissy, you are indeed a passionate woman. Do not waste such a thing on a man who hides the truth from you."

Be passionate with me, she seemed to hear, though he hadn't uttered those words. His eyes were so earnest, his words so blunt that she was taken aback. If she didn't know better she would have thought that Justin did care for her. But that couldn't be the truth.

She thought back to the young man he'd been those years ago. She'd been younger and she'd always thought him to be quite handsome, but he'd been so angry and caustic, and she'd been nervous around him all the time. He seemed less of all of that now. Oh, she still saw flashes of the anger heat his eyes, but he was able to temper it quickly. He had made peace with his father, with who Justin was. She envied him that, for she felt she was always trying to make peace with the person she was. And always falling short of the mark.

She thought suddenly of Rebecca, who would not have approved of her playing the piano with such transparent passion, let alone of her climbing into the carriage of a man on a moonlit night or allowing him to take such liberties with her. Again and again. She sighed. Why was it so very difficult for her to get things right?

"We are here now," he said.

It was the first time she realized the carriage had stopped. Voices, laughing and talking surrounded them.

"Go ahead, look," he motioned to the window of the carriage.

She gently pushed back the curtain to reveal the

sight outside. There at the edge of the Thames was a large warehouse of a building, a worn-out sign read *Rafferty's*. People were all around, women, clearly prostitutes judging by their shockingly low bodices and heavily kohled eyes, and men, gentlemen and lower classes all together. The women shamelessly rubbed against men as they walked to and from the gaming establishment.

To the right, against the far side of the building one man pressed a woman up against the wall, rocking back and forth into her while the woman clung to his shoulders. Clarissa's breath caught and heat surged into her cheeks.

When the man was done, he merely backed up away from the woman, adjusted his pants and walked away. The woman lowered her skirts and fluffed her hair, then moved back into the crowd to tempt another man. It was shocking, more than shocking. Clarissa had heard of such things, but she'd never really believed they were out there, just beyond her clean and tidy parts of London. And there in the midst of the crowd, an arm slung around one of the scantily dressed women, was George.

Her George.

He was dressed as he normally did, his clothes impeccably tailored, himself well-groomed. But his shirt had been opened and he wore no cravat and that woman rubbed her hand on the swath of his exposed chest.

Clarissa's own chest tightened and tears stung at her eyes. How could she have been so wrong about him? He'd been the perfect gentleman. For years they had been friends. For years he had treated her with respect. He had been charming, the perfect companion in every way. She would have sworn she knew him as well as she knew anyone.

"He has a penchant for fighting."

She heard Justin say, but she couldn't turn to face him yet, so she continued staring out the window. George gave the woman a big open-mouthed kiss and the thought that his lips had been on her own made Clarissa's stomach churn.

"Boxing is not all that scandalous," Justin continued, "but it would seem that he enjoys fighting outside of the ring as much, if not more, often goading men into fights. He's violent, Chrissy. I wanted you to see the truth for yourself."

If she'd been wrong in her estimation of George, then what did that mean for the rest of her life? More importantly, if Rebecca had been wrong about George, maybe she'd been wrong about everything. Maybe she'd been wrong in her estimation of Clarissa. Maybe the reason Clarissa struggled so much being a proper lady was because she simply didn't have it in her. Suddenly, everything felt upside down and backwards.

She swiped angrily at her tears, then moved back into her seat, pressing her back into the cushion. "Please take me back home."

"Chrissy, I'm sorry," he said.

"No, you're not." She felt a sudden burst of anger. Anger directed not at George, but at Justin. *He* had done this to her. He had revealed the horrible truth about George. And, she realized with a start, not just the truth about George, but about her as well. Time and again, he had stirred her passions. He had revealed her own true nature. Why had he done that? "This is precisely what you wanted me to see."

"Yes, I wanted you to see it, because I wanted you to know the man he really is. He is a man who has hidden his true nature from you. Do you think a man like that could ever be the husband you deserve?"

Her breath caught as a shocking idea occurred to her. Why had he done that? Did he have an ulterior motive she hadn't seen until now? She waited for him to say something else, for him to offer to be that husband she deserved, but he fell quiet. Finally, she let out a breath. "Take me back. Now."

. . .

They had not spoken at all the rest of the way back to her home. Clarissa had kept her eyes averted and concentrated on keeping herself from crying. Right now that was the only thing that mattered. She didn't want Justin to see her cry. Not for that. She felt like an utter fool.

He helped her back into the townhome and she found her way to the bedchamber. She called for her maid, made a silly excuse about falling asleep fully dressed and wanting to be more comfortable. The maid assisted her out of her dress and finally Clarissa was left alone. She went and stood at the window, looking out at the darkness.

It would be morning soon and she'd have to pretend as if nothing had happened tonight. As if she hadn't shared yet another passionate kiss with Justin Rodale. Pretend as if she hadn't spent time alone in a carriage with a dashing man. But most of all, she'd have to pretend that she hadn't seen the man she thought she wanted to marry carousing with a woman of ill repute, something he supposedly did on a regular basis. Justin had said George liked to fight. He'd never appeared violent to her; quite the contrary, he seemed rather docile.

Hot tears slid down her cheeks and she ignored them,

allowing them to come freely now. Is that what marriage to George would be like? She'd be at home waiting for him and he'd be out all night gambling and sleeping with other women? Certainly not. This was *her* George. She knew him, didn't she? And Rebecca had approved of him. Obviously, other maternal types did as well or there wouldn't be such a long list of women vying for his proposal. More than likely he was attempting to sow his wild oats until they married.

But what if?

What about all of those times she'd given him hints that she wouldn't mind holding his hand or having a longer than was proper embrace? And the kiss they'd shared? She'd initiated it, but then she'd pulled away when things had heated up too much. Because unlike Justin's heated kiss that slid desire through her body, once her kiss with George had intensified, she'd felt something alarmingly like fear.

It couldn't be fear of George himself, though. More than likely it was fearing what he'd think if he saw the real her. What would George think of the Clarissa that didn't always say the right thing, that felt the music too much when she played?

What if the entire reason George hadn't proposed to her was her? Had she worked too hard trying to be the perfect lady, behaved too properly? Had she been too buttoned-up and cold for him to find attractive? Rebecca had died before she'd been able to explain all that there was between a man and a woman. Perhaps she hadn't been wrong about George, but merely hadn't yet detailed to Clarissa everything there was about a man's needs.

When they'd dance, he'd told her on more than one occasion that she was the most beautiful woman in the room. But perhaps he was merely being polite, charming. Yet Justin was always able to elicit a passionate response from her. His kisses didn't make her feel nervous in the least. Perhaps he was right and it all simmered just beneath the surface and she merely needed a reason to let it out. She seemed to have little trouble with that in Justin's company. She knew George would never sneak into her house and find her bedchamber in the middle of the night. Perhaps there was a reason for that. If he didn't think his advances were welcomed, if he didn't think he'd find a passionate and willing lover on the other side of her door, there would be no reason for him to visit her.

But what if she kissed George again and allowed him whatever liberty he chose to take? What would he do? Perhaps it would change the course of everything. If she could share a kiss with George, as sensual a kiss as the ones she'd shared with Justin that might change George's mind. There was no reason to believe a kiss with one man over the other couldn't be just as passionate. Even more so because of her feelings for George. Then perhaps it would persuade George that she was a desirable woman. Then he wouldn't need to go and find and pay another woman for things that Clarissa could certainly learn to do.

She felt a momentary pang at the thought of Justin and the intimacy they'd shared in the carriage. There had been that instant when she had thought he might offer some sign of affection himself, but he hadn't. No, Justin was not for her. George was still the man for her.

She needed lessons in seduction and knew precisely who to ask to teach them to her.

Chapter Nine

Justin and his brother met for luncheon fairly regularly, and he was not certain today he'd be much company. His mind was otherwise engaged. Thinking about George Wilbanks, Rafferty's, and Clarissa.

All of Justin's other inquiries about the man had come up empty. Whatever else George did with his time, besides patronize Rafferty's, he was discreet about it. That was one thing in his favor. Justin had to wonder what the hell the man was doing courting her if he had no intention of marrying her. Perhaps their visit to Rafferty's last night had changed her mind about George.

Justin had hurt her, he knew that and he hated it. But he didn't regret taking her, revealing the truth to her. Were she to marry George she should at least go into such a union not being completely ignorant of her husband's behavior.

Roe was late, as was his custom. "People expect me to be late," he'd say. "I'm a duke." There wasn't much, other than cards, that Roe took seriously and he seemed to enjoy watering-down the title their father had so desperately loved. Roe knew he wasn't any different than any other man, any better than them. But he did enjoy toying with people.

Finally he arrived looking better than he had the other day, but still somewhat disheveled.

"You know, Rodale," he said as he removed his hat and sat at the table. "If someone coming into this club didn't know either one of us and was told that one of us was the Duke of Chanceworth, they would probably assume it was you. Why must you insist on showing me up?"

Justin glanced at his brother over his newspaper, then folded it and set it on the table. "I bathe regularly and have my clothes pressed. I hardly see how that is my showing you up. In any case, you're late."

It was understood that Roe would always be late and that Justin would always comment on it.

"Yes, shoot me. There was wretched traffic. Poor Lady Gramble lost a wheel on her new curricle and tied up all of Bond Street." Roe sighed dramatically.

The footman came and brought them today's fare, an earthy and aromatic lamb stew with hot buttered bread on the side.

"I'm not certain when I ate last, but this smells delicious," Roe said. He took a bite then swore loudly. "That's bloody hot."

Justin chuckled. "You should wait and let it cool."

Roe swore, but pushed the bowl aside for a moment. He crossed his legs and leaned back in his chair. "So tell me, what news do you have to tell me today?"

Justin stirred his stew, trying to cool the hot soup.

"Nothing. I am courting that girl and I suspect my attention is working to some degree. I'm told she danced with two other gentlemen the other night. And that a third asked if she would be attending the theatre later this week."

"Ah yes, how are you enjoying your latest foray into polite society?"

"It's entertaining," Justin said. They ate in silence for a few moments before Justin spoke again. "In particular the rumors about my lineage."

Roe looked up over the table. "Oh, now that sounds interesting." He tried another bite, and this one went down much easier.

"Yes, evidently my mother was French royalty. I overheard as much at a ball the other night."

"It could be true." Roe shrugged. "Don't suppose we know."

"It seems highly unlikely." Justin took a bite of his own stew and chewed thoughtfully. "And well, all the pertinent players are already dead."

"Unless *she's* still alive."

"My mother?" Justin certainly lived as if that were true. He'd been looking for her for years and until he uncovered her identity and found out for certain that she was dead, he would believe her alive. But he would not tell Roe that. "It's doubtful."

They ate in silence for a few moments before Justin spoke again. "I discovered that George Wilbanks frequents Rafferty's."

Roe whistled. "Are you still investigating him?" He held up a hand. "I won't ask, but I suspect it involves a certain fair-haired chit."

Justin grinned in spite of himself. "Rafferty's is not a

place for genteel women."

"Did he take said genteel woman there?"

"No." But Justin had. Guilt knotted in his stomach. What the devil had he been thinking to take Chrissy to such a place? Even safely ensconced in a carriage, what if she had been seen? He was the worst sort of ass. Still he hadn't known another way to show her George's true nature.

"Why don't you simply court the girl yourself and be done with it? Marry her and have little blonde, blue-eyed devils."

If only it were that simple. "You know I cannot do that. Clarissa deserves more than to be the wife of someone the likes of me."

"She could do a lot worse too, as you've discovered with the Wilbanks fellow. He might inherit a title, but with you she'd never want for anything. You have more money than God," Roe said.

"True." But he could never marry Clarissa, as appealing as that notion sounded. "How is the playing going?"

"Excellent," Roe said, allowing him to change the subject. He leaned forward, narrowing his eyes. "I've heard a rumor though. About a new player at Rodale's. Any truth to it?"

Justin nodded. "Ah yes, a young man. But he plays in the back room rather than the main floor."

"Is he any good?"

Justin nodded. "He hasn't lost yet." Ever since Clipps had brought the young man to Justin's attention, they'd been watching him carefully. So far he'd shown no signs of cheating. "Scrawny fellow, but he seems to be on the up and up."

"I want to play him," Roe said.

Justin shook his head. "You know that isn't going to happen. There are men on the main floor that would be none too pleased if I allowed someone from the back room to play among them. They are not interested in mixing with the servants and commoners."

Roe pointed his spoon at his brother. "You could make it happen. What is the use of having a brother who owns a gaming hell if he can't break the rules for me? It would be by special invitation from the Duke of Chanceworth."

"I'll consider it. But not now." Now his thoughts were filled of Chrissy and her lovely blue eyes brimming with tears as she'd begged him to drive her away from that filthy place.

• • •

It was nearly midnight when Justin heard the knock at his front door. He never required his staff to work late in the evening so he walked to the door himself. Besides any late night visitors he got were either women or men wanting to make a deal regarding their debts, neither of which his servants could manage.

He opened the door and there stood a woman, though her face was covered by a darkened cloak.

"Can I help you?"

She looked up then and he could see her eyes peeking through the darkness of her hood. Blue eyes.

"Chrissy?" He jerked her inside. "What the devil are you doing here? Are you deliberately trying to get me to ruin your reputation?"

"Of course not. I made certain no one saw me and in

this no one can see who I am." She flipped the hood off her face. Pink stained her cheeks from the cool night air. God she looked so beautiful.

He swallowed. "Come, we can talk in my study," he said. He turned and walked to the room, not bothering to see if she followed. Part of him hoped she'd come to her senses and returned to her carriage. He'd done his level best to resist her one too many times, tonight he could make no such promises. But when he turned around in his study, she stood near one of the chairs. "What do you want, Clarissa?"

She looked up, her lips parted. "You don't usually use my given name." She chewed at her lip, then slid out from under her heavy cloak. Beneath she wore a dressing gown.

He swore.

"Don't make this harder for me than it already is," she said, her voice shaky and unsure. "I need your help."

The nearly sheer fabric left little to his imagination. He couldn't see anything directly, but the outline of her every curve had lust pounding to his groin. Her shapely hips and narrow waist, the fullness of her breasts, damn but he wanted her. "Help is not what I have in mind when I look at you in that."

She smiled. "That is good news." Again she chewed at her lip, the motion both innocent and seductive, and the mixture was nothing short of intoxicating. He remembered the night in her bedchamber, his mouth on her breast, her unabashed response to him. His trousers became increasingly uncomfortable.

"I want you to teach me to be a seductress."

Justin sat in the chair to keep himself from either throttling her or teaching her how dangerous that request was. "You're going to have to give me an explanation."

"The other night, when you took me to Rafferty's, and I saw George, I realized something. He does not look upon me that way because he believes me to be too pure, too much of a lady. It is my understanding that most men want their women to behave the lady in public, but when it comes to the bedroom, they prefer, how shall I say this." She paused. "Harlots?"

He nearly laughed, but he couldn't manage a response of anything. She was still intent on marrying George. The realization of that was like a knife in Justin's chest, but he ignored the discomfort. If Wilbanks could not see the passion inside Clarissa, he was not only a cad, he was also a fool. "Who told you that?"

"It seems to be the general consensus." She came and sat in one of the chairs near his.

"How do you suggest that I instruct you to be a seductress?" It was a dangerous question. Would that he behave the perfect gentleman, he'd load her back into her carriage and send her straight home, as he'd promised her brother he'd do if she dared show up at his gaming hell again. Of course this was not Rodale's nor was it the first of her late night visits. And damned if Justin's own curiosity hadn't gotten the better of him.

"If I knew the specifics, I would not need your assistance," she said. "Rebecca died before she could explain much to be about the goings on between and man and his wife, the duties of the marital bed, as it were." She came to her feet and walked over to stand in front of him, her arms crossed over her body. She stood for a moment, then dropped her hands. "If I were a woman that you desired, one you planned an affair with, how would you proceed now?"

"First of all, this isn't about desirability. That, you already possess. Nor is this about duty, at least it shouldn't be. There should be enough attraction between husband and wife that the marital bed, as you called it, is pleasurable for both of them."

"What do you mean I already possess desirability? If that were true, then why did you walk away from me the other night? You said that it couldn't be me. That most certainly implies something is wrong with me."

He came to stand in front of her, gripped her arms. "Chrissy, take a breath. You thought I left because I did not want you?"

She nodded, exhaled slowly.

"Silly woman."

"Why then?"

"I'm not certain the truth is something I want to share with you."

She frowned. "I don't understand."

"It isn't right for me to tell you how much I want you when you are so intent to be another man's wife."

She opened her mouth and then closed it.

"I can, of course, explain matters of the flesh to you though. You said you want to be the seductress. In order to be that, you must be the one to take the action. If you want a man to kiss you, then kiss him first. If you want a man to touch you, touch him first," he said. "It is as simple as that."

She was treading on very dangerous territory and she didn't seem to see that. She might claim to be here because of some misguided attempt to seduce George, but the truth was she wanted Justin. He knew that, could see it in her eyes. She simply didn't know what to do with that desire because a union between them would ruin her plans.

Her skin was cool beneath the sheer fabric of her dressing gown. His eyes immediately dropped to her chest and he could see the faint shadow of her breasts, see the hardness of her nipples pushing against the fabric. The trick now was to see if he could teach her a lesson without losing control of his own desires because all he wanted to do right now was toss her down on the carpet in front of the hearth and plow into her, show her precisely how desirable she was.

He walked her toward the fireplace so that she could be warmed by the flames. She shivered a little, then nodded. "Thank you. Now then, I should simply kiss you?"

"Kissing is generally the way seductions begin, unless you'd prefer to verbally seduce me."

"Verbally seduce you?"

"Yes, you can tell me what you want to do to me and what you want me to do to you," he said.

"Oh my," she said, her voice full of breath. "I don't think I could do that."

"Clarissa, this really isn't necessary, I can assure you that you are a very desirable woman. If George cannot see that, he's an idiot."

She shook her head fervently. "No. I have no one else to talk about this with. I need to know what it is that a man will want me to do, how to please him."

"So kiss me," he said.

She looked up at him and for a moment seemed trapped in his gaze, her blue eyes wide and curious. She licked her lips and all Justin could think was that whatever George Wilbanks was doing at Rafferty's, he was a damned fool that he hadn't married this woman yet.

She took a step closer, placed one pale hand against his chest and lifted up on her toes. Gently, she pressed her lips to his.

The tentative, innocent touch of her lips was nearly his undoing. How could she affect him so without even knowing she did? Her exploration grew bolder, as her other hand crept around his neck. She pulled him closer, then opened her mouth to him. He kissed her back. He didn't need to be asked, he didn't require an invitation; she was the one who had shown up here wearing little more than her nightclothes and asking him to teach her the art of seduction.

He put his arm around her waist and pulled her closer to him, plastering her body, all-warm and soft curves, against himself. He cursed himself for still wearing his waistcoat and cravat. He wanted to feel her closer to him, wanted the sensation of her skin against his own. His hand slid down and grabbed onto her bottom and pressed her to him.

She released a little squeak of surprise, but never stopped kissing him.

"Clarissa," he said, pulling away from her. "You don't need to do this."

"I want to," she said. "I want to know what it is to seduce a man, to arouse him, to make him want me."

She was already well skilled in those areas, but perhaps it was best she not yet know that. He kissed her again, his tongue delving into her mouth, and she wrapped both arms around his neck. Her breasts, pert and soft with hardened nipples, grazed against his shirt. Damned clothes. He wanted to see her, but he didn't dare. He had to remain in control. He wanted to teach her a lesson, not take advantage of her naïveté.

He slid one hand up her torso, loving the soft feel of her body beneath his hand. He cupped one breast, weighing it in his hand. She did not have overly large breasts, but enough to fit nicely in his hand. Her nipple pressed against the fabric of her nightrail into his palm. Without another thought he slid his hand into the bodice, and finally, skin on skin. Her soft, burning skin against his palm. He shifted in an attempt to give his growing erection enough room in his trousers.

She moaned at his touch, kissed him more deeply, more passionately.

He stopped kissing her and moved his mouth to her jaw and then further down her neck to her throat, shoulder blade, nibbling and kissing as he made his exploration. Until he reached her and he sucked her nipple into his mouth, licked and kissed her breast. Her shocked moans filled the quiet of his study.

He wanted her. Badly. Right here. Right now. But this could not happen.

He abruptly stopped, stepped away from her. "If you want to retain your virtue, I suggest you leave. Now. I only have so much control." He didn't turn to face her, to see the hurt in her face, wonder in her lovely blue eyes.

"Justin, I…I am sorry," she said.

He heard her rustling with her clothes and when he finally turned to face her, she was hidden in her cloak. He walked her to the door and neither said another word as he put her back into the carriage and sent her to her house.

Son of bitch, he'd almost lost it, almost tossed up her nightrail and pushed against the wall and pounded himself into her until he'd been sated, and she'd known precisely what seduction really meant.

• • •

The following night Justin found himself once again in attendance of a ball. He'd already danced with Miss Riverton twice, and at the moment she was dancing with a wealthy, young earl. These men were a bunch of bloody fools if they needed to have one of them show interest in a woman before she was deemed desirable.

A tall man entered the ballroom, all smiles and charm. It took Justin a moment to realize who he was. He'd seen him a handful of times, most recently that night out the carriage window with Clarissa.

George Wilbanks. The biggest bloody fool of them all.

It was time to say something to him. Justin sized him up thinking on specifically what he'd say. What he wanted to do was resort to every dirty trick everyone in Society thought he knew simply to bring that man to his knees.

"If you will excuse me," he told Marcus, then he strolled toward George Wilbanks. He could see why Clarissa found him so appealing. He embodied what women tended to find attractive — tall, athletic, handsome with a gregarious smile.

As he approached, George turned in his direction. "Mr. Rodale, I'd been told you'd been introduced into Society, allow me to welcome you," he said congenially. The man seemed sincere, but Justin suspected he was just a damn good actor.

"Mr. Wilbanks. I've been wanting to make your acquaintance. It would seem we have a mutual friend." He fisted his hands, tempering himself else he lose what he had left of his civility and beat this man into a bloody mess.

"I suspect that in your line of work we have many mutual friends," George said with a grin.

"Indeed. But I'm thinking of a particular friend. Lady Clarissa Kincaid."

George's smile faded. "Clarissa is a lovely girl."

"Yes, she is. Might we converse more privately?" Justin suggested.

George nodded and the two men walked away from the crowd to a quieter area near some windows.

"You owe her an explanation," Justin said.

"I beg your pardon?" George's voice lost all hints of friendliness.

"She is under the assumption that the two of you are to be married. And now with this wager, and the fact that you're courting Clarissa and Miss Cooper. You need to remedy the situation."

George's lips quirked in a grin. "Yes, I cannot be responsible for a chit's romantic delusions. I can assure you it is not by anything I've said to her." He shrugged. "Yes, I have taken her on walks, danced with her. I enjoy her company. But I have never given her any indication I have any intentions toward her."

"You have never said to her that if the timing was right you would marry her?"

"I might have said something along those lines, but that is hardly to be considered a proposal," George said.

"You do, in fact, have to marry though. Your father has given you an ultimatum?"

"He has, but that makes no difference to me. I shall marry when I see fit."

He might say such a thing, but Justin was willing to wager that if daddy demanded it, George would comply.

"Your attentions are preventing her from allowing other suitors to pursue her."

George frowned. "She is a grown woman and does what she pleases, I can assure you that. Clarissa does not need my permission to find a suitable husband."

"She does if she's counting on you being that husband." Justin really wanted to hit him, right in his smug face.

"As I said, I spend time with many women. Clarissa and Miss Cooper included. It does not mean I am intending to marry any of them."

"You are leading them on," Justin said.

George met his gaze. "I like pretty things." His voice was cold and even.

The man was an utter cad, yet Clarissa seemed so convinced otherwise. "Have you told her about, how shall we say it, your hobby?" Justin didn't give him time to answer. "I've tried to enlighten her to some regard, but she misunderstood the situation." He wasn't about to tell the man that she intended to seduce him. Perhaps if he could convince George to tell Clarissa the truth, that he had no intention of marrying her, she would forget her seduction plan.

"To what are you referring?" George asked.

"Rafferty's." It was all that needed said.

"I see." Darkness crossed over George's features and gone was the congenial fellow and in the place stood a man who appeared quite deadly. "You told her about Rafferty's?"

"I did." No reason to mention he'd showed her as well. He still felt guilty about that.

"I don't see what business it is of yours. You certainly cannot think to marry the girl yourself. I don't believe bastard sons of dukes are suitable husbands for the daughter of an earl."

Justin felt his jaw clench, he fisted his hands, but knew better than to strike the man here. And from the looks of George's fists, the man was ready for a fight himself.

"I know Clarissa fancies me, it is a passing fancy." He shrugged again. "Or not, it really isn't my concern. Perhaps I'll decide to marry her some day, but perhaps I'll choose someone else. Miss Cooper is quite charming."

So while Justin didn't need to worry about George running away with Clarissa, he still had to be careful of what she would do. She was clinging to her sister-in-law's advice because it was that last shred she had. That one tangible thing she could do to make Rebecca proud of her, even from the grave. "The honorable thing would be to tell her the truth. Stop taking her on walks, stop pretending you're courting her when you have no intention of marrying her," Justin said.

"I never claimed to be honorable."

"Tell her. Or I will and with it the rest of your secrets."

George looked him straight in the eye, turned on his heel and walked away. Then the truth of the situation hit Justin in the face. What the devil made him think he could deserve Clarissa if he didn't believe George did?

He was a bastard by birth and a gaming hell owner. That was no life for a lady like Clarissa. Marrying her would sentence her to a life on the fringe of Society. He couldn't do that to her.

He didn't have any business being here among these people. He needed to get back to Rodale's and stay there. Tonight though he was here and he wanted one more dance with Clarissa. There was one more ball he'd agreed to attend, and then after that, he'd retire from this foolishness and go back to where he belonged.

Chapter Ten

Clarissa watched in horror as Justin crossed the room and spoke to George. And then the two of them walked off together to speak privately. Her heart pounded relentlessly in her chest as she watched. Was Justin telling George about her seduction plan? Was George telling Justin that she'd just kissed him in the garden and done so poorly? She wanted to run from the room, but her own morbid curiosity kept her feet locked to the floor.

"What are you doing?" Ella asked, suddenly appearing at her side.

"Sh," Clarissa said.

"Oh good heavens," Ella said. "Why are you shushing me? It is not as if you can hear them."

"I'm thinking," Clarissa said.

"You know this is good. Look, they are standing right there next to one another. What do you see?"

"Trouble," Clarissa said. "What do you suppose they're

talking about?"

"You, no doubt in my mind. Mr. Rodale is probably telling George to back off because he wants a shot at you. It's all wildly romantic," Ella said dreamily.

"Can you be serious, this is terrible. I have kissed both of those men." Then she looked at Ella in horror. "Oh you don't suppose they're discussing that."

"I don't know. I suspect you can ask one of them later. I'd suggest Mr. Rodale. Out of the two men, he seems the most honest."

"I believe I shall," Clarissa said. She walked off and headed straight for Justin now that George had left his side.

"Why were you just speaking to George?" Clarissa asked from behind him. Justin turned to face her.

"Clarissa," he said, his eyes warming as he took her in. "You look beautiful."

"Answer my question. What were you and George talking about? He looked very upset when he walked away. What did you say to him?"

Justin sighed. "Ask George yourself what we discussed."

Panic seized her chest. "Why won't you tell me? What did you do?"

"I did nothing more than ask him to talk to you."

"Justin, I don't need you to protect me," she said. Even now she wanted to lean up and kiss him. But of course she didn't dare, not here in front of everyone. Still the urge was overwhelmingly strong. But damnation he had gone and talked to George on her behalf.

"Whether or not you can see it, you need protection," Justin said. "I merely explained to George that it would be in his best interest for him to have a conversation with you about the future of your relationship. He is not the man you think he is."

Which meant that George could come up to her at any time and tell her that he had no intentions of marrying her. That he'd, once upon a time, been courting her, but over time he'd seen that she simply wasn't what he wanted in a woman.

"If you continue to talk to me alone like this, you will cause a scene. Dance with me," he said.

She chewed at her lip.

"Clarissa, trust me, I will not do anything to hurt you."

She looked up at his face, saw nothing but earnestness and honesty. She wanted to trust him. She nodded.

He swept her into his arms and for a moment she forgot everything she'd fretted about that evening—the failed kiss, Justin's confrontation with George. For a moment she was merely in Justin's arms.

She tried to ignore the feel of his large hand resting at the small of her back. She could feel the warmth from his palm and she remembered what that very hand had felt like on her bare skin. On her breast. Heat pooled between her legs. She swallowed.

"Tell me about your family," she said abruptly. "What was it like when you came to live at Chanceworth Hall?"

"Things were tense for a long time. I was angry with our father. He didn't treat me well, he clearly didn't want me there. But Roe's mother was always kind to me, treated me no differently than she did her son. I should say she treats me no differently."

"She is still living?"

"Yes, though she lives full-time in the country now with Roe's ward."

"Oh, that is right. I seem to recall Roe's ward and I came out the same year, but she did not stay for the full season. What is her name?" Clarissa asked. She was glad for the diversion, but couldn't help but notice how easy it was to converse with him. She was so intent on him being so very different from her. But he wasn't. They'd been raised the same.

"Caroline Jellico."

"She prefers the quiet life in the country, I suppose. I can see how that would be nice," Clarissa said. "Sometimes London is," she paused grappling for the right words, "too much." She sighed. How could she feel like that and ever be the right wife for George when he so clearly wanted, needed excitement and thrills at every turn?

"I enjoy the countryside myself. My estate is in Derbyshire," Justin said.

"Oh, I did not realize you owned an estate in the country."

"There was no way for you to know that," he said. "I bought it from a family who no longer could care for it, and I've been restoring it."

"I should like to see it sometime." She looked up at him, his dark brown eyes warmed.

"Of course."

She nodded and smiled, and they finished the dance. Once they were done, he leaned forward and kissed her hand.

"Can I come see you again tonight?" she asked in a whisper.

"Chrissy, I cannot say no to you."

• • •

Again there was a late night knock at Justin's door. And again

Clarissa stood there covered with her cloak. She stepped inside even before he invited her. His body reacted to her presence immediately, his abdomen tightened, a heaviness settled in his groin. He said nothing, but took her hand and led her forward.

Unlike her previous visit, he did not lead her into his study, but rather into the back parlor that led out to the garden. She lifted the hood off her head and took a deep breath.

"This room is lovely." Her eyes immediately fell on the piano that sat near the French doors.

"I was hoping you'd play for me," he said.

Her brow furrowed slightly. "Truly?"

He nodded. He helped her out of her cloak. "I've wanted to hear you play on an actual piano ever since you played that night on the pianoforte." If she left here tonight with her virtue intact, it would indeed be a miracle.

She smiled and sat at the bench. "What do you want to hear?"

"Whatever you want to play," he said. "Your favorite piece."

Her fingers settled on the keys and she began to play. He watched her as she closed her eyes and leaned forward, her fingers flying over the ivories. She was hypnotic to watch and the music itself was perfection. He'd bought this piano years ago because his mother had played and he remembered that as a boy. But it had languished in this parlor, empty of music.

Until now.

Until Clarissa.

Her body moved with the music, her eyes closed, her lips parted and she played and played, the notes soared and crested.

She held nothing back tonight. Her lips parted, emotion flickered across her face. She was so beautiful, mesmerizing the way she moved, the way she felt the music. He didn't understand why George didn't want her, why she wasn't enough for him, but right now Justin didn't give a damn about him. Though he was thankful the man hadn't yet claimed the lovely Clarissa.

Maybe someday he'd be able to convince her that she was more than enough for him, that he could take care of her in ways that George couldn't, that once he gave her a vow, he'd never leave her side. But she shouldn't have to settle, not for George and not for the bastard who so desperately wanted her.

"It's beautiful," he said.

Her eyes fluttered open and she finished the piece. "Beethoven's 22 Piano Sonata. It's not one of his more popular pieces," she said. "But it has always been my favorite."

He came to stand by her and she stood to face him. "What have I done so wrong that you keep sending me away?" she asked.

He pushed the bench out of the way, then pressed against her, putting his face close to hers. "You think you did something wrong?"

Her breath tightened. "Why else would you have stopped me? We were kissing and then you—" She swallowed. "You pushed me away." She looked up at him. "Do you not find me attractive?" She held a hand up before he could argue with her. "I know you have said you do, but you are a charming man, Justin, if I were truly desirable wouldn't you not be able to walk away?"

She did not mention George; she only wanted to know

if he found her attractive. He wrapped an arm around her waist and leaned into her. Her bottom brushed against the keys, the dissonance of the notes rang through the room.

"Clarissa, you shouldn't have to ask such a question. I find you exceedingly attractive. You're so beautiful that when you walk into a room, it as if all other women fall away and there is only you. I've stopped only because I don't want to ruin you."

Then he kissed her, showing her how much he desired her, precisely how attractive he found her.

. . .

Even as he kissed her, his words rang in her ears. "When you walk into a room, it as if all other women fall away." She had been told she was pretty before, but never quite like that. His kiss deepened and she nearly forgot why she'd come here tonight.

His kisses were intoxicating. Mesmerizing. And all the sensations she felt at his touch surged through her body. What was it about this man that made his touch and his kisses so very different from George's? She'd told herself that she'd come here tonight to find out why the kiss with George had not created such sparks in her body, but now, in this moment, she no longer cared. And she could no longer deny the truth—she'd come here hoping Justin would seduce her, hoping he'd make love to her. But then what would happen? He'd said it himself. He didn't want to ruin her. Ruination would mean marriage and obviously Justin had no intention of marrying her.

His hand slid up her dress, his palm against her stocking

clad leg. That touch purged her mind of all other thoughts, she couldn't think, could only feel. He stopped when he got to her knee, but the hidden part at the center of her begged for him to continue, for something she did not completely understand. With her sitting on the piano like this in front of him, she felt exposed, yet empowered. She opened her legs wider, pulled him closer to her.

He kissed her neck, nibbling at her throat. And his hand traveled upward from her knee to her thigh. She put her head back and focused on the sensations he caused with his hand, his mouth.

Her brief kiss with George had been without even a glimmer of passion. It couldn't simply be her skill level as she felt so different in the arms of this man. His mere touch brought awareness to her entire body, as if every nerve ending was alert, waiting for his command. One kiss with Justin Rodale and desire pooled to the center of her body, making her ache, making her crave, making her wet. His hand continued its climb up her leg and his mouth found her breast.

She arched into him. She knew she should probably stop him, should probably race out of her and return home, but she craved his touch too much. And like any good story, she wanted to know the ending, as she knew there was more to come.

He suckled at her breast, her nipples ached and his mouth gave her what she needed. And his hand, his fingers slipped in between the slit in her drawers to the curls that hid between her legs. The touch should have sat her upright, but this was what she'd been craving. This was where all the sensations hovered, over that center core. And he knew what to do.

His fingers parted her and every touch was like a jolt of pleasure. He toyed at the opening, running his finger around her and she tried to push against his hand, begging him for more. Every movement she made played notes and chords, creating odd music. And as he played her body, knowing every note to hit, her body crescendoed, climbing higher and higher and his mouth kissed her breast and his hands pushed her closer and closer to her peak.

Finally she broke. Notes sang out from the piano. She cried out, calling his name again and again. "Justin!" She shook in his arms as the pleasure rode through her.

When it was done, he picked up her body, cradling her to him and carried her over to the plush blanket in front of the hearth. They lay down beside one another. She snuggled against his chest, wishing his clothes were removed so she could touch his skin.

This man was a mystery to her. Her body craved him, yet at the same time she feared her need of him, her reaction to his touch.

"You want me to teach you these things so you can seduce George," he said. His deep voice broke through the silence. "But what if I want you all to myself? What if I only want you to do these things with me?"

• • •

After an hour of lying in Justin's arms, Clarissa made some excuse about needing to get home before daylight. Once in her room and settled in her bed, she lay there, looking up at the darkened ceiling, her mind racing.

Over and over she heard his words: "What if I want you all to myself? What if I only want you do these things with me?" She was so confused, and being next to him with his hands on her body, she'd wanted to say, "Yes, I pick you." But she couldn't do that. He hadn't offered marriage, he'd merely told her he wanted her. That wasn't enough.

It wasn't so much what he said that terrified her, but her reaction. She'd wanted to roll over and agree. Tell him he could be the one. She'd come so close to giving him her body and then where would that have left her? Justin wasn't bound by the same societal rules as she was. If he ruined her, there was nothing that demanded he do right by her and marry her.

It was time to settle things with George once and for all before she did something she truly regretted with Justin.

He was illegitimate, and he owned a gaming establishment. Not at all the manner of man she was raised with the idea of marrying. Nor did he have intentions of marrying her. He'd even said once that he'd never marry a girl in proper Society. No, George was the kind of man she was supposed to marry.

It didn't matter that all things considered she'd pick Justin.

Chapter Eleven

On very little sleep Clarissa had risen the following morning for a scheduled shopping excursion with Ella. Her brief stop in the dining room to pilfer a piece of something for breakfast had been met with Marcus and Vivian sitting entirely too close to one another for the first meal of the day. They'd exchanged pleasantries, but Clarissa hadn't stayed around for any lengthy conversation.

Once in the carriage with Ella and Lady Weaver, they both began talking so quickly Clarissa wasn't certain who to listen to.

"Start over," Clarissa told them.

"Mother, allow me," Ella said. Her mother nodded. "I cannot believe how much you missed. This will teach you to leave a ball that early. Lord Rutherford announced his engagement to an heiress. An American heiress."

"Good heavens, wasn't he already betrothed?" Clarissa asked. "To Jane Pendergast. I thought they'd made a love match."

Ella nodded. "Yes, I believe they were in love. Evidently, he and this American girl got themselves locked in a room at some soiree and the girl is obviously ruined though even she said that Lord Rutherford never touched her. Still he's doing the honorable thing by marrying her. I'm told poor Jane is simply devastated."

"He is a man of good breeding, doing the right thing by the American girl," Clarissa said.

Lady Weaver nodded. "True, but I don't believe the Americans put much stock in their reputations else the girl would not have been out without a chaperone. Let this be a lesson to you girls."

"Yes, mother," Ella said. She gave Clarissa a sly smile.

Clarissa smiled in return, but she couldn't help wondering what would happen to Jane Pendergast. Would another man step forward to marry her now that she'd had her engagement dissolved? Yes, it was a good thing that men of title did the honorable thing, but it still seemed a little sad considering Lord Rutherford and Jane had seemed quite enamored of one another.

Right now Clarissa knew if she allowed her heart to choose, she'd be back at Justin's house tonight. There was no denying that she had feelings for him and that he clearly desired her. But she couldn't afford to fall into another scandal with him. There were those that wouldn't have survived the rumors that had surged after Clarissa had visited Justin at his gaming hell. Thankfully, Vivian had smoothed things over and Clarissa's reputation had remained unscathed. It was one thing to dally with a gentleman knowing he would be honor-bound to marry you, but to engage in an affair with a man who had no said obligation was downright foolish.

"Sounds like a very exciting evening," Clarissa said. She'd almost asked Justin Rodale to make love to her so anything Ella or her mother had to tell her seemed to pale in comparison.

Ella shook her head. "An understatement, and I still can't believe you missed it. Where were you?"

"I went home early with a headache."

Ella looked at her with a slight frown as if she did not believe what Clarissa said. But she would not inquire further in front of her mother. They arrived on Bond Street and began their shopping. It didn't take too long for Clarissa to hear several different versions of the story from the night before. Everyone was talking about it.

Ella was able to sneak over to Clarissa while her mother talked to the milliner about a new hat. "Where were you?" Then she paused and her mouth opened wide. "Were you out kissing George? Oh, or Mr. Rodale?"

"I did kiss George, though not last night," Clarissa said quietly. She hadn't yet told her friend the details of her kiss with George because so much had happened. And she still didn't understand her own reaction to said kiss.

"And?"

She had thought she loved George, once upon a time. Well, she was still fond of him, she knew that much. Though now when she thought of love, George was not the first name that came to mind. Everything had seemed so concrete in her mind a few short weeks ago. Now it was all muddled. But what to tell Ella? Clarissa wasn't generally in the habit of lying to her friend.

"Your silence tells me everything," Ella said. "Your

heart knows what it wants, Clarissa. There is no reason to deny it."

"I'm not so certain it's that simple. What if what my heart wants, my heart can't have?" Then she shook her head. "There's no reason to answer that." Regardless of the pull she felt to Justin, they could never be. Theirs was not the kind of love match she'd read about in Jane Austen novels. Clarissa was no Elizabeth Bennet, and Justin was certainly no Mr. Darcy. If anything he was more like Mr. Wickham.

No, no he was far more honorable than that.

Yet she felt certain that if she pursued Justin, she would end up ruined and heartbroken. Whereas George would do the right thing, he would have to, he was the heir to a viscount. People knew he'd courted her. Not only that, but it had become quite clear she could no longer trust herself with Justin. If he asked her those questions again, she might say yes. Not that he'd asked for anything permanent. No, she had yet to be able to evoke that manner of response from any man. Perhaps she merely hadn't done it the right way.

It was time for her to take action. If she was to marry George, she needed to give him that extra push to make the commitment. Tonight's ball would be the perfect time. People would still be reeling about recent events. It would be all anyone was talking about. Until tonight.

Until Clarissa Kincaid compromised herself.

• • •

Everything was planned to perfection, and even though the entire scenario made Clarissa feel slightly nauseated, she felt certain it would all work. By the end of the night she should very well be engaged. She scanned the ballroom looking for her future intended. He stood across the room next to Ella's brother and two other gentlemen. They had glasses in their hands and held them up every now and again in an almost salute to one another. Men were strange creatures.

"Are you quite certain you want to go through with this?" Ella whispered next to her.

"Yes, it is the only way," Clarissa said.

Ella shook her head vehemently. "Not true."

"What are my other options?"

"You could *not* marry George."

"He is the man I'm supposed to marry. We're a perfect match." Or at least they were supposed to be the perfect match. She'd spent so much time believing that, could she question it now? Especially in light of what she'd seen of George. Still, Clarissa intended to follow Rebecca's recommendation. She knew from experience that her own personal instincts left much to be desired. So despite her doubts, Clarissa intended to adhere to her late sister-in-law's suggestion.

If she were to rely on her own choice, she'd end up married to a gaming hell owner, not at all a suitable choice for a lady. Besides, she'd been pursuing George her entire adult life—she couldn't turn back now. If she walked away from George, then who was she? What did she know of herself if she didn't know that she was meant to be his wife? And who would she marry? There weren't any other men lining up to pursue her. She wasn't eccentric enough to be a successful spinster.

Ella shook her head, her perfectly coifed curls bounced with her movement. "I don't think so. I don't believe you suit at all. You're vibrant and funny and I hate to see you waste your life married to him. I don't trust him."

"You're only saying that because you've known him forever. Since you were a girl. You don't know him the way I do." But even as she said the words, they felt false to her.

"Well, you'll certainly be able to say that after tonight." Ella eyed her. "I wish you would reconsider, but I know you and once you have your mind set, nothing will change it. I will help, as I promised I would, but know that I'm not happy about it."

Clarissa swallowed hard and nodded. "Duly noted. I promise to do the same someday when you set your cap for some gentleman I don't approve of."

"How do you know that will happen?"

"I know you and no doubt you'll fall for some poet who has no income and doesn't like to wear undergarments."

Ella's eyes widened. "My goodness but you've become rather worldly."

Clarissa turned her attention back to George. When he came to retrieve her for his dance, Ella was supposed to send him to meet her elsewhere. The room she found was perfect and no one would be the wiser. It wouldn't even take a kiss or a touch. Once they were found alone together, she'd be compromised. George would be urged to marry her. He'd come to his senses and propose.

Now was the time. She looked at her friend. "Wish me luck," she said.

"Most definitely." Ella grabbed both of Clarissa's hands and looked her straight in the eye. "I'm not leaving you in there for very long. I don't want him to ravish you. Oh, Clarissa, do be careful."

Clarissa squeezed her friend's hands and nodded. She

made her way to the room where she was to meet George. It was a billiards room, but one that was apparently no longer in use. Lord Wooten had recently purchased all new billiard tables and had moved them into a larger room upstairs, leaving this smaller room completely unused.

There were currently three billiard tables in the room and it looked as if they'd also brought in some unused chairs stacked against the far wall. There was a door at the other end of the room that she assumed led into a closet. There were no windows and no one had passed through the corridor outside while she had stood there earlier in the evening.

It was perfect. She would grab his attention by letting him know that she knew of his favorite game. Then when Ella found them alone, he would do the honorable thing and marry her.

George was a good man.

She paused, considering what she was about to do. Never did she think she'd be one of those women who trapped a man into marriage, but she needed to do this before she did something with Justin Rodale she couldn't undo. Once she was officially betrothed to George, then she and Justin could simply be friends.

She had been so close to asking him to make love to her the other night. She'd so wanted it, with him, but that was the terrifying part. She was supposed to be with George. Not Justin Rodale. Rebecca had never cared for Justin; she'd always said he was too surly. Of course that wasn't the way he was now, and Clarissa couldn't help but wonder what her dear sister-in-law would think of Justin the man. She didn't have long to consider it though as the door creaked open.

"Clarissa, are you in here?" George asked. He poked his head in and saw her. "What are you doing in here?"

"I thought you might enjoy seeing what I'd found in this room." She motioned to the tables behind her. "I'm told they're quite old and worth something to collectors."

He stepped into the room and closed the door behind him. He paused. "No chaperone?"

"No, it's just me. But no one uses the room, so we're safe."

He moved forward to the table and stopped at one in particular. "Mahogany wood, good detailing." He moved around each side. "All eight legs seem sturdy and the pockets are in excellent condition. Very interesting. I was not aware Lord Wooten was an avid billiards player."

"Oh, I hear he's terrible, but he doesn't know that," she said.

George laughed. He picked up one of the cues. "The leather tips seem to be original. Clearly Lord Wooten doesn't actually play very much." He ran his hand against the wood of the table, then the top. "Why the sudden interest in billiards?"

"I am interested in you and therefore interested in what you like. You do favor this game?"

"Yes, I do." He narrowed his eyes at her playfully. "Have you been spying on me?"

Well, she had, but not that particular past time. "A woman never shares her secrets."

"It's hard to believe that you would have secrets, Clarissa," George said. "You're a lady of upmost values."

"Every lady has secrets. Don't let any of them tell you any differently." She shrugged. "I suppose it depends on what manner of secrets, though." They could only talk for so long.

"I must admit I'm wondering if Lord Wooten would be

eager to sell them to me," he said.

It was on the tip of her tongue to tell him that he shouldn't be making large purchases if he owed someone else a large sum of money. But she was still unsure if that had been a complete lie or if he did in fact owe someone money.

"Did you want to go and finish our dance?" he asked.

"No." She walked over to him and looked up at him. "I was thinking we could do something else."

"Do you want me to teach you to play?" He gave her a wicked grin and a shiver slid over her body. Not the delicious sort, but the sort that made her feel uneasy, nervous.

He took her by the hand. "Come here, let me show you something."

She took a deep breath and allowed him to pull her near. If she were going to be compromised, she supposed it didn't matter if she was found simply in a room alone with him or in an embrace. He pressed his mouth to her in a surprising kiss. He'd pinned her body between his and the billiard table.

He slid his knee between her legs. "You are a seductress, Clarissa Kincaid. I would never have known. It's a nice surprise though." Then he kissed her again.

She wanted this, she reminded herself. She wanted to be George's wife, was destined to be so.

His mouth left hers, but trailed down her throat. His warm mouth did little to excite her. "Tell me you want me, tell me you want me to touch you," he said roughly.

She nodded. "Kiss me," she whispered. "I want you to kiss me," she said.

"Clarissa Kincaid," the female voice sounded from the door. But it was not Ella's voice. They had been caught, but not at all by a friendly face. Clarissa's heart fell into her shoes. She held her breath as she turned slowly to see who it was. It was Lady Wooten. But George would step forward and say something to save her, to salvage her name. He'd claim they were betrothed. The room was deafeningly quiet. Clarissa turned back around to find George had slipped out behind her through the other door.

Clarissa opened her mouth, but found she had no words.

"What are you doing in here, young lady, of all the scandalous wanton behavior." Lady Wooten shook her head disapprovingly. "I am just, I mean I never would have expected it from you." The woman's eyes narrowed in on her. "Let us go and find your brother. Right now. Who was that man with you, Clarissa?"

Clarissa took one last look at the door behind her. George had abandoned her. The weight of her faulty decision crashed down upon her and she found it difficult to breath.

"Well, you can tell your brother. I'm certain he'll make the man do the right thing. You should be quite thankful that I came in when I did. Whoever that man was that was in here with you would most certainly have taken advantage of you and by the way he quickly exited, he wouldn't have seen to it to marry you." She pat Clarissa's hand. "Perhaps your brother can take care of the situation for you, though. Brothers can be quite persuasive when it comes to the honor of their younger sister's."

She continued to chatter on while she led Clarissa back into the crowded ballroom. All Clarissa could do was focus on breathing. In and out. In and out. Everything seemed to be moving slower than usual. The people they walked by, their words blurred, the music sounded broken apart, and there was a strange wooshing that pulsed inside her head.

She needed to sit down.

Whether he intended to or not, George had just compromised her. And then he'd left. If he'd cared for her at all, he would have come forward then. If he had had any intention of ever marrying her, this should have forced his hand. And yet, he had run. She had been utterly wrong about the nature of his character. Worse still, Rebecca had been wrong. If she couldn't trust in Rebecca's guidance, what could she trust in?

"My Lord, if I could have a moment of your time," the woman said.

Marcus turned to face her and he caught one sight of Clarissa and brought his arm around her. "What happened?" he asked her.

But she didn't get a chance to answer as Lady Wooten was already talking. "I walked right in on them. Not sure who the man was, though, he scurried out as soon as he could. I do believe her virtue is in tact, though it might not have been had I not entered the room when I did. If I were you I would find out who he was and demand he make right of this."

"Thank you for your help," Vivian said. "Clarissa, let's get you home."

Well, she had ruined her reputation, but she wasn't engaged. In fact, she was utterly ruined and more than likely Marcus would send her to the country to save the family any more embarrassment. Two scandals in one year was more than any family could handle.

Chapter Twelve

Justin had seen everything from across the room. His companion rattled on about wagering odds of hazard, but he was not paying him any attention. Instead he'd seen the hostess lead Clarissa across the ballroom and straight to Marcus and Vivian. They had, in turn, escorted her immediately out of the building. Something terrible had happened.

And then Justin saw George Wilbanks step back into the room and glance around. He looked far too suspicious. Justin knew that Clarissa was not thinking correctly and hell if he hadn't scared her last night. There was no telling what Clarissa would attempt to do.

"If you'll excuse me for a moment," Justin said, then walked away from Baron Flick. He moved quickly and caught George by the arm. "What the devil happened?"

George pulled his arm away. "I do not need to have any unwarranted attention from you."

"Answer my damned question or I'll give you more

attention than you'll be able to recover from. What was the matter with Clarissa?"

George looked away from Justin, then back to him. "She made a bad decision and now she will have to deal with the repercussions."

"Did you violate her?" Justin had to physically hold himself back because he was damn near ready to throttle the man. It wouldn't be an easy fight either. They had nearly the same physique and Justin already knew George enjoyed a good fight.

The man's jaw clenched. He met Justin's gaze. "That is none of your damned concern. Now unhand me before I have you tossed out on your ass. I don't care if you are the brother of a duke." He jerked his arm away, then straightened his jacket.

"So she is ruined and you deserted her."

George met Justin's gaze and stared back unwavering. "I will not be trapped in a marriage I do not want."

Justin turned on his heel before he pounded the man in the face.

He might not deserve Clarissa himself, but damned if he'd stand by and allow her name to be ruined. The life he could offer her wouldn't be what she'd dreamt of, and she'd likely not be accepted back in the crowd that had always accepted her. He didn't have much to offer her, but if she'd have him, what he did have he'd gladly share with her.

• • •

Clarissa sat in the front parlor of her house while Vivian and Marcus talked about her a few steps away. "I'm right here and I can speak for myself. Stop whispering and speculating and simply ask me what happened."

Marcus and Vivian stopped talking and turned to face her. Vivian stepped forward. "Of course you're right, Clarissa, we're very sorry." She looked at Marcus. "Come and sit."

He complied and they sat across from her on the settee. "Whatever has happened, we'll weather it, as a family," Marcus said. "Again."

She smiled. "I appreciate the support, honestly I do," Clarissa said. "But in truth, this is all my doing, completely my fault, my choice." She shook her head. "I'm a fool."

"Can you tell us what happened?" Vivian asked gently.

"In my desperation to marry, I recklessly and ruthlessly attempted to compromise myself." She laughed, her voice sounded foreign to her own ears. "And I suppose it worked." She tossed up her arms in defeat. "I am officially ruined."

Marcus shook his head. "Seems to be a bit of an epidemic lately."

Vivian patted Clarissa's knee. "It has always been the way. Women are forced into lives where we have no choices. We're told whom we must marry and we're often sold off to the highest bidder. London is a pot simmering and it's about to over boil."

"Lovely metaphor, my dear," Marcus said.

"Yes, well, it is the truth. And the man in question?" Vivian asked.

"It was me," a male voice said from the door.

Clarissa looked up to see Justin standing in the entrance to the parlor. His presence was enough to start the wellspring of tears she'd thus far been able to hold off. "No, Justin, don't."

"*I* ruined her and *I* will marry her," Justin said, ignoring her protest.

Marcus came to his feet. "We've been friends for years, Justin, but if you defiled my sister, I might be forced to hurt you."

"Oh stop it." Clarissa stood. "All of you. I know you all mean well, but my goodness. Ever since you've returned to London, Marcus, this entire family has surrounded itself with my actions and tried to fix everything. The fact of the matter is I went to see Justin that night because George told me he owed him money, which as it turns out is a complete lie because all of his gambling is done not at Rodale's but rather Rafferty's, a horrific place down by the Thames." She took a deep breath. "In my utter insanity and drive to marry George, I mistakenly believed him to be an honest man, a true gentleman. I ignored everyone's warnings. I was so afraid of what choices I might make outside of him, and I tried to coerce him in to marrying me and he walked out. I honestly can't say that I blame him. No one needs to pick up the pieces of my mess in an attempt to clean it up. I made a mistake, I shall endure the consequences."

"So you were in the room with George?" Vivian asked. "You tried to compromise yourself?"

Clarissa took a deep breath. "I thought that if George and I were found alone together, it would be enough. He, as it turned out, had other intentions. That was when Lady Wooten found us." She gave Justin a weak smile. "It was George. Justin is simply being noble." Tears stung the back of her eyes. Oh how she wished she wouldn't cry.

Marcus shook Justin's hand. "I am thankful I will not

have to hurt you. I am rather fond of you."

"I still wish to marry her. We've been seen together; everyone will believe it was me. We can simply say we were already engaged."

"You were never courting me though," Clarissa said. She'd longed for a proposal from Justin, but not like this, not in a forced situation. "I'm certain everyone knows that, if they've even been paying any attention. No one would honestly believe — "

"That you would lower yourself to be wooed by me?" Justin asked sharply.

Clarissa met his gaze, anger burned in his amber eyes. "No, I was going to say that no one would believe that a man such as yourself would be interested in a woman the likes of me."

Vivian stepped forward. "Perhaps a discussion meant for later." She smiled warmly. "Let us all sit and we can have tea and decide how to proceed. Because regardless of what actually happened tonight, Clarissa, your reputation is now damaged beyond anything I can repair. Especially in light of my own actions as of late."

Most people had accepted Vivian even after her public admission of being a fallen woman, but there were still others who had not been so forgiving. Marcus called for a tea tray and added brandy to the list for himself and Justin.

"I am willing to marry her," Justin said again. "But I will not beg you," he said to Clarissa.

"I was a fool. Just as you told me I'd be and just as Ella warned me. I didn't listen to any of you. George is not at all the man I thought he was." So now she was brought to the reality that she had a difficult choice. She could resign herself to living in the country or she could marry Justin, a man she knew had no real interest in marrying anyone in society. A man who desired her, but didn't love her. A man who was far more honorable than she'd ever given him credit for. Funny, she had resigned herself to marry George knowing he didn't really love or want her, believing he would follow through merely to satisfy his honor. That she had been prepared to do; however, it was a good deal less palatable now that the man who didn't love her was Justin.

Some women could bounce back from these situations. They might live a bit on the edge of Society, but they became mistresses, well cared for ladies who picked lovers based on the sorts of gifts they could receive. But she could never be one of those ladies. She simply wasn't sophisticated enough for that. So she could decide right now to be a spinster or to be Mrs. Rodale, the wife of the bastard son of the Duke of Chanceworth. She hated even thinking that way. She didn't consider Justin's birthright. He certainly proved to be nobler and more gentlemanly than George ever had.

"Clarissa, this is your decision. Whatever you decide," Vivian said.

They weren't going to make her marry him. She looked over at Justin. She could have done much worse for herself, and at least she knew one thing—she would never think of the duties in the marriage bed as tasks to be endured because she desired Justin with every fiber of her being.

"Yes, I will marry you."

• • •

The following morning, Vivian pulled Clarissa aside as she

came down the stairs.

"Your brother is still asleep, but I should like to have a conversation with you," Vivian said.

"Thank you," Clarissa said.

"Let's sit in the front parlor." Vivian grabbed Clarissa's arm.

In such a short amount of time Vivian had become like a sister to her. She hugged her tightly. She missed Rebecca and her guidance. More than likely had she still been living Clarissa would never have gotten herself into such a mess. Perhaps if she had counseled with Vivian, she would have listened.

They walked into the parlor and Vivian sat on the settee. "I suspected you might want to talk a little. About what happened."

Clarissa sat. "I'm not certain there's anything to discuss. I made a poor choice and now must live with the consequences. A series of poor choices, actually."

"Can I ask you a question?"

Clarissa nodded. "I don't suppose I have anything to hide anymore."

"Do you love George?"

"No, I don't. I thought I did at one time, but I think I was trying to convince myself that I loved it."

"Then why so determined to marry him?"

Clarissa recounted the story about Rebecca.

Vivian nodded and gave Clarissa a warm smile. "So you believed your own judgment not good enough?"

"It never was." Clarissa shook her head. She told Vivian about Christopher, a story she knew Vivian would understand more than anyone else. "So you see, my own judgment has always gotten me in trouble." She released a short laugh. "I suppose that is precisely what happened here too."

Vivian patted Clarissa on the knee. "You were trying to do what you thought was best. It would seem that George pretended to be a good man whereas Justin is a good man. There is a difference."

Justin was a good man, an honorable man. Why had it taken her so long to see that herself? Well, she knew it now, would be reminded it of it every day. She'd be his wife. A wife he never loved. She took a deep breath. "Then I suppose it is for the best that Justin and I are to be married."

"He will make you happy in a way George never could," Vivian said.

Clarissa knew that that was the utter truth. Yet at the same time Justin could do something to her that George never could—break her heart. But there was nothing to be done about that now.

"Thank you for talking to me," Vivian said.

For so long she'd been certain she would have made George a good wife. Obviously, the bond between them hadn't been enough to change him. It hadn't been enough to change her, not in the way that her relationship with Justin had changed her. No, George Wilbanks would never be her husband.

Instead, she would be Mrs. Justin Rodale.

• • •

One day later she was a married woman.

She and her new husband stood on the sidewalk waiting for their carriage. The few friends and family members who had attended the brief ceremony had already departed. Clarissa hadn't wanted a party. At least not yet. She didn't deserve one.

The weight of the ring on her finger felt foreign. She looked down at the band encircling her finger. It was beautiful with the filigree details and the fiery opal stone at the center.

"Do you like it?" Justin asked.

Clarissa looked up at him, slightly embarrassed he'd caught her staring at the bauble. "I do. Very much."

"The stone reminded me of you, polished and shiny on the outside." He took her hand and held it up to the light, turning her hand slightly. The opal blazed from within. "See that, that is how I see you. That fire inside." He released her hand. The carriage pulled up alongside them and stopped. It was, by far, the finest coach she'd ever seen.

Justin helped her inside, then took a seat, not across from her, but next to her. Her husband. He would be by her side for the rest of her life now.

"Where are we going?" she asked.

"I want to show you something."

They rode along in silence for a while until the rig stopped and Justin once again assisted her down. She looked around and noted the street looked much different in the daylight than it had that fateful night she'd come here alone. Unlike the worn sign at Rafferty's, Rodale's sign was freshly painted and tasteful.

Justin took her hand. "Come," he said.

"Inside?" she asked.

He nodded. "This belongs to you now too."

She hadn't expected that. She allowed him to pull her up the stairs and then opened the door and she stepped across the threshold. It was not overly busy because of the time of day, but there were more people here than she had expected. The same man she'd spoken to that first night approached them. Instead of the grizzled frown she'd been greeted with that night, he wore a broad smile.

"Mrs. Rodale," he said and then grabbed her into a fierce embrace. "Welcome to Rodale's."

"Thank you," she said. She couldn't help but smile at the unexpected warmth of the man she'd thought to be an ogre.

"Clipps, this is Clarissa. Chrissy, Basil Clipps. He essentially runs this place," Justin said.

"Mr. Clipps," she said with a nod.

"Nah, you call me Basil. My wife will be wanting to meet you soon."

"We can arrange a dinner," Justin said. "I'm going to show her around. Anything of note today?"

Clipps shook his head. "The young man was back again last night. Your brother is becoming more and more insistent that we let him play the boy."

"I'll see to it," Justin said. He took her hand again and led her forward.

The room was large and divided up into sections, she supposed based on the type of game played there. Heavy wood tables made of the finest mahogany were placed around, and surrounded by matching ornate chairs. Lush red draperies hung from the windows blocking out the sun, but the room was well-lit. There were a few doors off the main room and then a staircase that led upward.

"That door over there," Justin said pointing to their right, "leads to the kitchen and there is a dining room there. We serve food whenever people want to eat. I hired the cook from Lord Abernathy's estate."

They made their way to the stairs and climbed to the top. Once inside, she saw the windows that overlooked the playing floor. "You can watch from up here," she said.

"Indeed. We don't catch cheaters very often, but it happens. And I like to stay informed."

The office had plush furnishings, all the finest materials, like she would find in any wealthy family's home. "It's all very lovely."

"I wanted you to see it," he said.

"Why?"

"Partly so you could see what I have built. And partly because you are my wife, this business is yours as well."

She shook her head in confusion. "Am I not simply to manage your household?"

"You are welcomed to do that, but I might want your input for other things. Remember I know about Mr. Bembridge and his talents. He has not salvaged the finances of two families in London. He's developing quite the reputation. There are men twice your age who would not have made such sound decisions. You have a unique mind for business, Clarissa. This is our business."

She looked around at everything. The wife of a gaming hell owner. Or as Justin declared, part owner of a gaming hell. This was certainly not the life she'd imagined. For the first time in her adult life, she was thankful Rebecca and Charles and her parents were dead. They would be appalled at what her life had become.

A handful of weeks ago, it had been a scandal for her to stand on the sidewalk outside of this establishment and now she was inside, shared a name with it. So much had happened, she barely recognized herself. And, yet, those familiar feelings of excitement welled up inside her. Her entire life she'd had to fight her own nature to fit into the mold of the perfect society lady.

At least now she didn't have to. No one would be watching her anymore. She could relax and simply be Clarissa, the wife of the gaming hell owner.

"I took the liberty of responding to your invitation to the Potterfield ball tomorrow night," Justin said.

She nodded. "It will take some adjustment, I suppose, not attending such events, but I shall get used to it."

Justin shook his head. "Chrissy, what are you talking about? Marrying me does not mean you can no longer attend parties. I didn't bring you here as a way of telling you this would be your new evening pastime. You are my wife, I shall attend whatever party you wish to go to and Mr. Clipps will manage things here until I arrive."

"You wish to take me to balls and soirees and the like?"

"I don't want you to change your life because you've become my wife. You do still wish to be part of Society, do you not?"

She looked up at him, but said nothing for a moment. "Why would you want to do that?"

"Do you not want me to? I was under the impression that you enjoyed such functions," he said.

"Of course, I'm merely confused as to why you would want to join me. Many of those people have been nothing but rude to you," she said. Were it her, she probably would be glad to never see those people again.

"Are you ashamed of me?"

She swallowed the lump in her throat. "No, of course not.

I merely meant that—" She waved her hand dismissively. "It is of no consequence what I meant. Of course we will attend parties together. I am your wife." But this meant that she was not done trying to be the perfect lady, and to make matters worse, now she would have to do so for the both of them, which would not be easy. She'd heard people say wretched things about him before, but as his wife, she'd be damned if she'd allow that kind of talk.

Chapter Thirteen

Clarissa stood in the room that was now her bedchamber. Justin's townhome was not much different than her family's, but this was the adjoining room to the master bedchamber. This was where the lady of the house slept, where the wife slept.

She was the wife. The weight of everything that had occurred in the last few days hadn't yet settled on her. Or at least she hadn't yet been able to work through everything as of yet.

After her tour of Rodale's, they'd come home, and had a delicious dinner in a small private dining room. After that he'd asked her to play for him again, but this time he'd kept his distance, preferring to listen to her from a chair. Admittedly, the playing had relaxed her some, but she did have to wonder if now that they were married, his desire for her had somehow waned.

The door opened and she jolted. But it was not Justin, instead a maid.

"Pardon me, my lady, my name is Mary and if you'll follow me, Mr. Rodale thought you might enjoy the adjoining room better," she said with a slight curtsey.

Clarissa nodded and followed the girl. It was odd that Justin would send for her to come to his bed, rather than simply come get her himself, but she was unsure of how these things should work. But instead of leading her into another bedchamber, the maid had brought her into a bathing chamber. It was a small room, covered in wood paneling and there in against the wall sat a large white tub with metal claw feet.

"I took the liberty of filling it with warm water for you." She pointed to a small table next to the tub. "There is a tray there with scented soaps and hair rinses. Whatever you should need. There is also a bell if you find you require some assistance."

Clarissa took everything in. Her family's townhome in London was very nice, and Ashford estate in the country equally so, but she had never seen a bathing chamber before. "Thank you," she said.

"May I assist you out of your clothes?" Mary asked.

"Yes, please. A bath sounds quite lovely right now." It would seem that Justin had thought of everything. She looked around the room whilst the maid worked on her buttons. There was another door on the opposite side of the small room. "Where does that door lead?" she asked.

"To Master Rodale's chamber."

So this is what separated their rooms. A shared bathing chamber. Was that common among married couples? She did not know since most houses were not yet equipped with such rooms. After Mary had unpinned her hair, Clarissa swept it to the side and put it in one long braid.

Once she was undressed, the maid held her hand and helped her into the deep tub. Warm water lapped at her as she settled inside its wet cocoon. Tension melted off her. She tilted her head back against the metal edge of the tub and closed her eyes. After the door had closed, she took a peek at the various bottles on the tray. Rose water, lavender oil, lemon soap, whatever she could have wanted right at her fingertips. She took some of the lavender oil and poured a few drops into the water. The sweet perfume wafted over her, relaxing her further. Again she settled into the water.

She wasn't certain how long she lay there. A door opened and she looked up expecting to find Mary there to assist her out, instead Justin stood over her. His amber eyes took in the length of her. Though submerged in water, he no doubt could see her every curve.

She resisted the urge to cover herself. He was her husband and therefore had every right to look upon her body. "This is lovely," she forced herself to say. It was not untrue. The room was a pleasant surprise.

He smiled. "More lovely than I could have imagined."

Heat flooded her cheeks.

He came to stand beside her, picked up her braided hair. "May I?"

"Of course."

He methodically unbraided her hair. She sat up so that her shoulders and breasts were above the water. He retrieved the pitcher. "Tilt your head back," he said. Then he poured the warm water over her head.

Chills started in her scalp and ran down her body raising the tiny hairs along her arms and tightening her nipples.

He massaged soap into her hair, his fingers working up a lather. She closed her eyes and reveled in the sensations. He'd obviously chosen the lemon soap as the citrus smell soon surrounded her. And then he was once again pouring warm water over her hair to rinse out the soap. Her scalp still tingled from his ministrations. She wrung out the water from her hair and re-braided it so it hung in a long damp chain.

"Are you ready to get out?" he asked.

"Yes, the water is getting a little cold now."

He opened a cupboard and pulled out a blanket, then went back over to her and wrapped her in it as she climbed out of the tub. The blanket cocooned her in warmth.

"Come," he said, and he held a hand out to her.

. . .

He pulled her into his bedchamber. His mouth met hers in a hungry kiss and he forgot all about the situation of their marriage. They might have married out of necessity, but that didn't change his desire for her. And now she was his. Only his.

Her tongue slid against his and his erection pressed painfully against his trousers. God, how he wanted this woman. They kissed for several moments. He reached between them and pulled the blanket off her. It slid to the floor. He tilted her chin up so he could see her face. He grabbed hold of her shoulders. His hands ran up and down her arms. "You want me, Chrissy, don't you?"

"Yes," she whispered.

He took a shuddering breath. She'd alleviated most of

his concerns in that one answer. He supposed there would always be part of him that wondered if she'd wished George had been the one to marry her. Justin knew he didn't deserve Clarissa Kincaid, but damned if he didn't long for her to want him.

He took a step back to see her, admire her body. Everything he'd seen in the bathtub had been through water. Right now, in this moment, it was pure Chrissy and he wanted to take his time and memorize every curve of her body.

Her breasts were perfectly shaped with rosy nipples that budded for his pleasure. His eyes followed down her torso past her waist to her curvaceous hips. He didn't let his gaze dip any further, not yet. With one hand he twirled her around so her backside faced him. "I'd ask if anyone has ever told you that you have a delicious bottom, but I'm fairly certain I know the answer already," he said.

She looked over her shoulder, her brows angled in surprise. "I've always thought it was a little too big."

He ran his hands over the rounded flesh. "I disagree, it's perfect." While his hands continued to fondle her generous bottom, he nibbled at her neck. Looking up, he realized they stood directly in front of his dressing mirror. Clarissa's head leaned back against his chest and her eyes were closed in an expression of delight.

He pulled his hand back, then swatted her bottom playfully. Her eyes flew open and he waited for her reaction. She didn't cry out in pain, instead a shy, yet sexy smile slid into place that had him itching to take her right now.

His eyes took in the full length of her and he was certain in that moment he'd never seen a more beautiful woman. She was perfect in every way.

He swatted her bottom again and she cried out this time, but with pleasure.

Now. He wanted her now. There was time later to take things slow and easy. He kissed and suckled her neck while he removed his trousers and shirt until he too stood nude before the mirror. The contrast in their skin was mesmerizing. Hers so creamy white compared to his darkened skin covered in dark hair.

He led her to the bed, allowing his hands to continue to play all over her body eliciting moans from her. They stood next to the bed, but he didn't lay her down yet. If he did that, it would be over too soon. This night would only happen once; he wanted it to be as pleasurable for her as possible.

He reached around her body and cupped her breasts as he nibbled the tender flesh at her neck. She leaned back against him, her bare bottom pressed against his erection. He looped one arm around her waist and held her close to him.

"I want you, Chrissy," he said against her ear.

She nodded, but had no words in response.

His hand slid down her stomach. She sucked in a breath. His fingers parted between her pubic hair and he found her slick with want. He closed his eyes to try to reign in his own desire so he could last for her, have time to pleasure her.

He turned her swiftly so he could kiss her again. She met his kiss with a fierce passion, a passion only for him. This woman, she was his perfect fit. He lifted her gently and put her on the bed, then climbed on beside her. She smelled of lavender, lemon, and desire.

He kissed her. His finger found her wetness and the tiny nub and he moved against it.

She parted her legs further opening herself to him. "Yes, yes," she hissed.

He positioned himself atop her and moved to her opening, then kissing her gently, he pushed himself into her. She was slick for him, so tight.

"Oh God, Chrissy."

He kept his hand between them moving against her while she adjusted to his invasion. When she raised her legs, wrapped them around his waist, he knew she was ready.

Gone were his thoughts of trying to take things slowly. He pushed in and out loving the deepness of her. Faster and harder he pushed until he heard her yell his name then saw her clench the sheets while her body shook with her release. It only took one more thrust before he spilled his seed. He leaned against her back for a moment listening to her heavy breathing and quiet moans. He'd never felt desire this intense with any other woman.

He lay down beside her, pulled the coverlet up to their waists. He traced his finger along her collarbone.

"That made me feel a little bit sinful," she said with a delicious grin.

"Nothing sinful about it. We are married now." He pulled her against him so her head rested against his chest. Something in that moment felt so right he nearly stood to leave, but he forced himself to stay where he was. He couldn't run any longer. Not from Chrissy. She deserved better.

And while she'd deserved better than him, she had married him so he'd have to prove to her and everyone else that he could be a good husband.

• • •

Clarissa stirred her tea and listened to Ella's mother, Lady Weaver, catalogue all of the fashion mistakes from the soiree they had attended the previous evening. She had been invited over to their house for refreshments that afternoon and Clarissa had welcomed the outing. She knew that it was Ella's way of letting her know that simply because she had married Justin did not mean she was no longer welcomed in their home.

"I don't know how it's possible for Eleanor Banks to find that many dresses in so many shades of green. And she doesn't look good in any of them. It's a mystery," Lady Weaver said. She tapped her spoon onto the side of her teacup, then took a sip.

In the carriage on the way here, Clarissa had decided what she must do. She could not stand by and allow people to say disparaging things about her husband. It had been one thing when they'd been friends, but now she bore his name. She had an obligation to support him. She thought back to the evening she and Ella had overheard that conversation about Justin and the mystery of his mother's identity. The women discussing it had been quite nasty. But if it was true, what one of them had said, that Justin's mother was French royalty, if Clarissa could prove that, then it might change how people saw him, how they treated him.

She considered exactly how she would ask her question, but she knew if there was information on Justin's mother, then Lady Weaver would know, or at the very least know whom they could ask.

"How was the wedding, dear?" she asked Clarissa.

The night she shared in Justin's bed with filled her mind. She felt the heat of blush in her cheeks and she brought the teacup to her lips. "It was quick, nothing too exciting. I suppose that's the way when you have a rush marriage." She had spoken too quickly, jumping from one sentence to the next. "Thank you for inviting me over for tea."

Ella eyed her suspiciously, but Clarissa merely smiled in return.

Now was as good a time as any so her friend wouldn't pry in front of her mother. "I was wondering. Several nights ago Ella and I overheard a conversation about my," she took a breath, "husband."

"Yes, yes, handsome devil, that one," Lady Weaver said. "Consider yourself lucky to have snagged him."

Snagged him, as if their marriage hadn't been the result of a damaging situation. As if Clarissa had merely caught his eye, he'd courted her, and proposed like a true gentleman. "Yes, well, these women the other evening were discussing the identity of his mother and one of them suggested she was French royalty." She took another sip of her tea and did her best to sound casual. "Have you ever heard such a thing?"

"Well, let me think. He looks to be about six and twenty or so." She tapped her fingers on her skirt and the muffled drumming made Clarissa nervous. "I do recall there being a large group of French nobles that came here to escape from the war. That would have been in the late 40s, I believe." She nodded as if agreeing with herself. "Yes, that's right, they were having another revolution in France, you see. We had several French families that came and stayed and attended many Society functions." She frowned. "I can't recall any of them being royalty though. I'm certain I would have remembered a princess."

"But they were here in London?"

"Oh yes, at least for a Season, perhaps two. Many of the women, Englishwomen, that is, weren't too keen on the visitors. They thought the French women were intent on stealing all of the men." She took another sip, then waved her hand. "Poppycock, it was. Only one of them married an Englishman. Lord Forrester, his wife is French. But the rest," she waved her hand around, "they all went back to France, I suppose, once the revolution had settled down." She tilted her head. "I hadn't yet met your father yet, Ella, but it was the end of that Season that he took notice of me." She smiled warmly.

"I suppose one of those women could have been his mother," Clarissa said.

"Now remind me again who his father is?" Ella's mother asked. "I know he's illegitimate," she said in a whisper even though the three of them sat alone in her own drawing room. "But I can't place him."

"The Duke of Chanceworth. His brother Monroe is now the duke, but they shared a father," Clarissa said.

"Ah yes. Now let me think, I never did garner the attention of any dukes, but I do remember him. Dashing, powerful yet he always seemed so stern. I believe he was betrothed to Millicent, or perhaps they were already married then." She shook her head. "I wish I remembered more."

"You've remembered plenty," Clarissa said. So now she knew that more than one French woman had been in London during that time. Any one of them could have had an affair with the duke and gotten pregnant with Justin. Lady Forrester might be just who she needed to talk with to uncover more information.

• • •

They sat in the carriage on the way to ball. Clarissa fidgeted with her hands, the satin of her gloves felt as heavy as wool tonight.

"What did you want to ask me?"

Clarissa looked up at Justin. "I beg your pardon?"

"Earlier today you said you had something you wanted to ask me, then the messenger arrived and we never continued the conversation."

Clarissa took a deep breath. "Was your mother really French royalty?"

He shook his head. "I don't know where that rumor got started, but no, she was not French royalty."

"People talk." She shrugged. "I don't recall you ever speaking of her, so I didn't know. And I figured, as your wife, that now we should get to know one another better."

"My mother, or the woman I knew as my mother, Eloise Rodale, was a music teacher, or at least she had been before I was born." His words were even, almost as if he spoke of someone he knew rather than his own life. "She was not, as it turns out, my actual mother, only the woman who raised me until her death. That's when I went to live at Chanceworth Hall."

She was quiet a moment, thinking on his words. Had he been devastated when he'd found out the woman he'd lived with since infancy hadn't been his mother? The urge to embrace him nearly overwhelmed her, but she stifled it else she really cause damage to her name. "But your other mother, she could have been French royalty?"

"That's highly unlikely."

"You do not know who she was?" she asked. She watched his features, the way his jaw tensed and how his knuckles whitened as his hands squeezed into fists. "At all?"

"I do not," he said.

She'd inadvertently hit upon a sore spot for him.

"Not for lack of searching though. I've been looking for her, or rather her identity, for years."

"I could help," she said.

He gave her a sideways grin. "Help me find my mother?"

"Yes, I'm certain I could prove useful."

"Why would you want to do that?"

"I am your wife," she said, hoping that was enough. She certainly empathized with him. She knew what it was like to grow up without a mother. "I never had a mother," she said, "not really. Rebecca was there for me as was Aunt Maureen, but even though I never met her, I've always missed my mother."

He eyed her for a long while as if estimating whether he believed her or not. "It's very sweet of you, Chrissy, but there's nothing you can do."

Chapter Fourteen

Justin led Clarissa into the ballroom, her arm linked with his. Hell, he hadn't wanted to come to this thing tonight, but he knew it was important for Clarissa's sake. If she disappeared from Society now, it would only breed more contention and rumor surrounding her compromise and their marriage.

He knew what it was like to live at the fringe of Society and he didn't want that for her. So he fully intended to go with her to whatever party she wanted to attend and he'd dare anyone to say anything untoward about her or to her.

He didn't know where her interest in his mother had come from. But he suspected she might want to discover that his mother was, indeed French royalty in an effort to make Justin himself seem more noble, more worthy to be among the rest of them. He suspected, though, that should they ever uncover his mother's identity, Clarissa would be sadly disappointed.

• • •

It was their first outing as a married couple and to say Clarissa felt waves of nervousness was a gross understatement. She had no way of knowing how she would be greeted, or what everyone was saying since her compromise. Did people believe it was she and Justin who had been caught in an embrace that night, or would she be brandished a fallen woman? She wasn't certain if Justin's name was enough to protect her from the sharper tongues of London.

The conversation in the carriage on the way here about his mother had not gone as well as she'd hoped. Perhaps she should have been more gentle when bringing up the information about his mother, but how was she to know that he'd been lied to his entire life?

She'd, at least, seen a photograph of her mother and had heard her brothers speak of her. Clarissa knew she favored her mother in coloring, if not temperament. But Justin, he had nothing save what someone had told him and she had ripped that away from him. She sighed.

Perhaps if she brought him some information, something concrete, then he'd see how helpful she could be. Tonight she would speak to Lady Forrester, see if she could get additional information from what Ella's mother had told her. She didn't want to desert him when they first arrived, but she was eager to find Ella. She made a quick excuse once Justin was safely surrounded by Marcus and Vivian and Aunt Maureen.

Clarissa spotted Ella and grabbed her arm. "I have been waiting for you forever," she said. "Come with me."

"Where?"

"To speak with Lady Forrester."

Ella grinned broadly. "I'm pleased to see you are following up with matters concerning Mr. Rodale's mother."

That gave her pause. Perhaps this was not the most appropriate task for her to pursue in light of the fact that he hadn't seemed too keen on the idea. But if she could uncover his mother's identity for him, that would be worthwhile.

Justin had been kind enough to insert himself back into Society, a place she'd always assumed he hated, in order to support her. She owed him. Yes, that was most certainly why she was looking into the identity of his mother.

"Have you ever met Lady Forrester?" Ella asked.

"Yes, but it was years ago. Haven't spoken to her since," Clarissa said.

"Well, we simply cannot walk up and ask her which French woman had an affair with the Duke of Chanceworth."

"Of course not. We shall have to be more delicate." As they approached the woman, Clarissa hoped that delicate manner would come to her because at that very moment, when Lady Forrester turned to look at them, Clarissa didn't have the slightest idea of what she would say.

Both she and Ella curtsied.

"My lady," Ella said. "My mother was telling us the most fascinating story the other day."

Thankfully Ella had more wits about her. Clarissa smiled. "Yes, about the revolution in France when many of you took refuge here in London."

Lady Forrester smiled in return. "*Oui*, it was when I met my amour," she said. Though age had grayed parts of her red hair and lined parts of her face, she was still a beautiful woman. Her green eyes shone brightly and her smile spoke of genuine friendliness.

"There were others of you that came?" Clarissa asked.

"Oh *oui*, there were perhaps twenty of us." She frowned. "Mostly girls and a few of our parents or chaperones. The men stayed to fight or protect their properties, but we came here for protection, and we had a glorious time."

"Did you know all of them?" Ella asked.

She nodded. "Yes, most of us grew quite close. Some of us still correspond with letters. And then I wasn't the only one who stayed here in England."

Clarissa's stomach jolted at the news. Perhaps Justin's mother had stayed here in England and was still here, all these years later.

"Let me see. Juliet moved to Brighton as she loved the seaside there, Celeste went to medical school and became a doctor. Mercedes also stayed, but I'm afraid she died from the fever last year," Lady Forrester said.

"I'm very sorry," Clarissa said.

"Thank you, she was a dear friend."

"That must have been quite difficult, trying to find places for all of you to stay during the height of the Season," Clarissa said.

"No, not at all. We all stayed in the Manchester House. It was lovely. Lady Manchester was a widow and she had opened her grand home up as a hotel and we all lived there together. She was wonderfully hospitable."

Clarissa and Ella looked at each other and smiled. Manchester House, it was still a hotel. Clarissa knew where it was.

"I suspect you were not the only one who found love while you were here," Ella said.

"Ah, no, amour was all around." She laughed.

"Anyone fall in love, but not get to stay as you did?" Clarissa asked.

Lady Forrester's eyes narrowed. "What are you asking, my dears?"

Clarissa looked at Ella and gave a little shake of her head. They could not come right out and ask or else risk starting rumors anew. While Lady Forrester seemed kind and unassuming, they did not know her and therefore could not trust her with such information. "Nothing, we merely thought it was such a romantic story." Clarissa feigned a giggle she hoped sounded authentic enough.

Lady Forrester smiled. "You shall find love, my dears, in time." She motioned for them to come closer. "I have such fondness for you English, but English ladies are taught to wait on the gentleman. If you know you have found the right one, you go after him."

Clarissa and Ella walked away, arm-in-arm.

"If I had my eye on someone, I would take her advice," Ella said boldly. "I think she's right. Why should we have to wait on the men?"

"But it can also get you into more trouble than it's worth," Clarissa said.

Ella squeezed her friend's hand. "True, but in the end I believe you married the best man for you. In time I hope you'll agree with me."

• • •

They had been home from the ball for nearly half an hour. Justin had tried to give her time to undress, have the maid take her hair down. He rapped his knuckle against Clarissa's bedchamber door.

"Come in," she said.

Justin opened the door. Clarissa sat at her dressing table, brushing her hair. She smiled shyly at him. He stepped inside her room and closed the door behind him.

"Do you need help?" he asked.

"No, I'm nearly done." She brushed a few more times, then methodically worked her hair into a long braid that went down her back. She stood and faced him. She removed her dressing gown, leaving her in nothing but the sheer shift he'd purchased for her. He took in the sight of her.

His mouth went dry.

"Do you like it?" he managed to ask.

"I do, it's very soft." She ran her hands down the gossamer fabric, it moved like water across her perfect body. The sheer fabric hugged her curves. "Do you like it?" she asked in return.

He met her gaze. "Indeed. It is why I purchased it for you. I knew you would look stunning in it. I was not wrong." He took several steps toward her and she met him the rest of the way.

"You will be a good husband to me, Justin," she said.

Her words echoed through him, words he never thought he'd hear, at least not from her. "I shall try. Every day, I shall try."

She slid her arms up around his neck. "I thought tonight, I would." She chewed at her bottom lip. "That is to say, I thought I would take your advice. You asked me once or suggested that you be the man I use my seduction on." She smiled. "As it turns out you were training me for you."

"Do your worst, Lady Seductress," he said. She began

working at his buttons of his shirt. Once they were all undone, her warm hands slid across his chest, down his abdomen. The muscles there tightened beneath her touch.

She slid the shirt off his shoulders, down his back and onto the floor. She leaned in, placed a kiss on his chest, her mouth tentative at first and so soft. She grew more brazen with each kiss until she nipped and licked at him. He closed his eyes, focusing in on her every touch. God how he wanted this woman as he'd never wanted another.

Her fingers dipped into the waistband of his trousers ever so slightly. Her mouth found his, slanted across him, her tongue swept across his in an invitation he could not ignore. He kissed her back eliciting a feminine groan from her throat. Her fingers slid lower into his pants, brushing across his erection. Then her hand was gone and she pulled back from the kiss.

"My apologies having never unfastened a gentleman's trousers before. I should like to see what I'm doing," she said with an impish grin.

It was a slip, the word she'd used, but it warmed him from the inside. *Gentleman.* Oh, how he'd wish that were true. If only for her, he wished he'd not been a bastard, not been the product of an affair so he could offer his sweet Chrissy a good name.

She unfastened his pants and slid them down his legs, then worked on his undergarments until he stood before her without a stitch of clothing. "I should like you on the bed now," she said boldly.

"Indeed." He followed her orders.

"Now then, tonight I believe I shall have my way with you."

"I am but a vessel for you to enjoy," he said.

Her eyebrows rose. She climbed up on the bed with him, still wearing the nightrail he'd purchased her. It moved flawlessly with her, flowing over her body like translucent silk.

"I like this," she said, trailing her fingers along the hair that started at his chest and tapered down his stomach. "It is like a map."

He chuckled. But as she bent and kissed along the trail, his laughter died in his throat. She was his. His and only his. Her fingers shimmied up his legs lightly all the while her hot mouth blazed kisses across his abdomen.

"Chrissy, you're torturing me," he groaned.

"Patience. I am the seductress."

Then her mouth was on him, lightly at first, explorative. But when she took the length of him, he grabbed the sheets. Again and again she brought him closer to the edge. Then she stopped. She slid her body up his, the soft fabric tickled across his skin.

"I fear I have loosed a monster."

She laughed. She met his gaze. "Perhaps. I do hope you don't mind."

"Never."

Then she sat astride him. She pulled the nightrail off her body, tossing it onto the floor. Her breasts begged for touch. She settled herself on him, without allowing him entrance. The moisture from her desire slid against his erection. She moved against him, her eyes fluttered closed and she tilted her head back.

Damnation if she wasn't testing his restraint. His hands cupped her breasts and she moaned in response. Her release hit quickly, her eyes shot open and she cried out. Then just as quickly, she sat up and slid herself down on top of him.

She was impossibly wet. Tight. Warm.

There was no hesitation in her movements. She took what she wanted and gave him more in return. He felt his release building. So when she climaxed again, he let go, spilling himself inside her.

His and only his.

She moved to lay next to him, her head nuzzling on his chest.

"I don't think you need any more lessons."

She laughed. "I had a most excellent teacher."

They were quiet for several moments before she spoke again. "Did you know there was a group of French nobles who took refuge here in the late 1840s during the revolution?"

"Am I now to endure a history lesson?"

Clarissa moved so her chin rested on his chest and she could see his face. "Quite the contrary. I thought you would find that of personal interest."

"And why is that?" He braced his arms behind his head.

"You are seven and twenty, are you not?" When he nodded, she continued. "Then you would have been conceived sometime in 1848, about the time the French visitors were here."

"Clarissa, what are you talking about?"

His use of her given name meant she'd gotten his attention and not necessarily in a good way. "Your mother. Don't you think she was probably one of them?"

He shook his head. "No, my parents met in Paris."

She frowned. She'd been so certain after speaking with Lady Forrester. "How do you know that?"

"I was told that."

"But don't you think it's possible whoever told you that didn't tell you the truth? It's far too much of a coincidence that so many of them were here during that very time. I know where they stayed too."

"Why are you doing this?" he asked, all manner of flirtations and his easy nature gone.

She dipped her finger in the divot right below his throat. "I merely want to help you find your mother."

"Yes, but why?"

She sighed. "You endeavored to put yourself out here, in Society, to help me and my situation," she added quietly. "Then you rushed in and married me when I made an utter fool of myself. It is the very least I can do." She looked up at him. "Plus, I know what it is like to not know your own mother."

He sighed. "Where?"

"Manchester House."

He stood from the bed, retrieved his clothes. "I shall look into matters." And just like that he strode from her room, entering the door that adjoined hers to his. It closed behind him.

She'd effectively seduced him and then just as effectively, it seemed, built a wall between them. She rolled over on her back. Why was she doing this? To prove to everyone that he was just a worthy as they were to bear a title. She wanted everyone to see him as she saw him, not as a bastard, but as a true gentleman. A man full of honor and character.

• • •

Everything Clarissa had told him last night had given him pause. After he'd left her bed he'd gone down to his study and written out a handful of notes, sending out queries to check on a few things. This morning he'd already heard back from two of them. It would seem the little bit Clarissa had discovered certainly changed everything in regards to his search for his mother's identity.

The woman whom had raised him, the one he'd loved and thought was his mother until that fateful day when she'd sat him at the table and told him everything. Or what he'd thought was everything. As it turns out, he wasn't quite certain of anything she'd told him. It was funny, though, he felt no anger towards her, no bitterness. She'd been a good woman, no doubt having her hand forced by the men with power who stood invisible behind her.

Eloise had told him that his parents had had a brief affair in Paris and that his mother had been unable to take care of him.

He'd spent all of his resources investigating a time when his father had supposedly been in Paris, a time when his parents could have met and had their brief affair. And then Clarissa had brought to his attention something he'd never quite considered. What if his parents had met right there in London? If his mother had been there, that changed everything.

So far he'd confirmed that there had, in fact, been a large group of French nobles who had come to London for refuge during the last revolution. And the timing fit perfectly for his birth. It certainly explained why he'd been raised here in England rather than in France. He'd also discovered that Manchester House was still opened and acting as a hotel, though the ownership had changed.

Now he had to decide if he wanted to pursue this particular thread. He'd followed every other lead he'd ever come across and they had all led to nothing, simply one dead-end after another. But this, this was so very different than anything he'd ever looked into, which made him wonder if it wasn't the truth.

Clarissa poked her head in the doorway of his study. "Are you working?"

He closed the letter he'd just read. "Did you eat breakfast?"

She nodded. "Your cook is wonderful. Did you steal him away from some unsuspecting lord as you did for Rodale's?"

He grinned. She was making an effort, discussing neutral ground as a peace offering. "I did not. She's actually Mr. Clipps's wife's sister. And you're right, she is a very good cook."

Clarissa came in and sat opposite his desk. "Justin, I did not mean to be insensitive about your mother. I merely wanted to help."

He wanted to ask her again why, why she was so intent on helping him. She'd given him a reason last night, but he knew there was more to it. But he didn't want to hear her say the words or to lie and say something else. He knew that if she could prove his mother was of noble birth that it would somehow make it right in her eyes that she'd had to marry him. It would make him more palatable to her. "I looked into your claims," he said.

Her brows rose in surprise. "Already? And what did you discover?"

"Everything you said was correct. At least about the group of nobles staying in London." He tilted his head.

"Now whether or not my mother was one of the women that was here, that I do not know."

"But you intend to find out?"

He nodded. "I do." It would seem he'd made his decision. He would pursue this until the end.

"How?"

She wanted to help him, he could see it in her eyes, the way she chewed at her bottom lip. If finding out the truth about his mother would somehow reconcile for her the fact that she'd married a bastard, he would help her. He only hoped that what they found out didn't make matters worse. Justin stood, braced his palms on his desk. "A visit to Manchester House."

"I wish to accompany you on that visit," she said.

"I suspected you might."

She frowned. "And?"

"There's no reason for you to go."

"I want to help. I found this particular clue, it would seem I've earned a place at your side for this."

Earned a place at his side. The words warmed his insides like a much needed meal after a long day's journey. He exhaled slowly. "You may come along, on one condition."

"Anything," she said. She came to her feet, met his gaze.

"When we discover that my mother was nothing more than a French commoner promise me you won't be disappointed."

"Why would I be disappointed?"

"I require a promise."

"Very well, I promise. When will be leaving?" she asked.

"After luncheon."

She turned to leave, then paused. "Oh, Ella is joining us for luncheon today. Could she accompany us to Manchester

House?"

"Why?"

"She has helped me find the information thus far. It was her mother that gave me the first clue. It seems only fitting that she…never mind, it is not of importance."

"Yes, she can go." If the girl would offer a buffer should they discover less than pleasant news about his mother, then he would welcome her company.

• • •

Ella smiled at the two of them in the carriage. The good thing about having someone else in the carriage with them though is that they did not have to discuss last night and the fact that he'd left her bed. When they'd married, he'd fully intended for them to spend every night in the same bed. But last night he'd had to leave, hadn't been able to face her in light of the things she'd said about his mother.

"This shall be an adventure," Ella said cheerfully.

"I want it to be productive," Justin said.

She gave him a serious nod. "Indeed, Sir."

Clarissa smiled. "Were it not for Ella's mother, I'm not certain we would have stumbled upon this clue," she said again, this time for Ella's benefit.

"My mother knows nearly everyone in town," Ella said. "I've asked her to remember if she saw any of the visiting women with your father." She shrugged. "But that was the Season my father started courting her and she said she was addle-brained for months."

She was endearing this one, Justin could see why Clarissa was her friend. She was genuine and happy, a good sort to be around when you tended to take matters in life too seriously. "I thank you for your assistance," Justin said. "I have been searching for my mother's identity for many years."

"I'd wager you never thought your two accomplices would be the likes of us," Ella said with a giggle.

Clarissa clicked her tongue. "It is not proper for a lady to make wagers, Ella." Then she grinned. "Well, except for that one lady." She met Justin's gaze.

"Who?" Ella asked.

Clarissa shook her head. "I cannot say. It would not be the thing. Rodale's is nothing if not discreet."

Justin smiled.

Ella twisted her mouth and hit her hands upon her lap. "Oh you two and your secrets. No fun at all."

Justin chuckled. "To answer your question, Lady Ella, no, I never expected to have two ladies as my accomplices." The carriage rolled to a stop and he assisted both women down from the rig. "I would appreciate the two of you allowing me to do the talking."

Clarissa nodded. They climbed the steps to Manchester House. It was an attractive hotel, converted from a rather large corner townhome. The lobby greeted them with light blues and yellows, fabrics and wallpaper that was probably a few years past its prime, but still in good condition.

He motioned to the two of them to sit in some of the cushioned chairs in the middle while he went to speak to the man standing behind the counter. It was not an overly large lobby so Justin felt certain everyone in the room would be able to hear his request, but nothing could be made of that.

"Yes, how may I help you, my lord?" the man asked.

"Simply a mister. I should like to speak with you about

records of past guests."

The man retrieved a book from beneath the counter and set it in front of Justin. "This contains the last year."

"No, this would have been from a long while ago. 1847 or 1848," he said.

The man shifted his weight. "Yes, well, that would be when my cousin owned this property." He returned the book to under the counter.

"Do you still have the records, Sir?" Justin asked.

The man waved his hand, shaking his head. "No, no, that would be far too much trouble and I am quite busy," he said.

Clarissa looked around the empty lobby. She stepped forward. "Yes, well, since you are so busy, might we look for you? You could simply point us in the right direction."

The man stood there, not saying anything for several breaths. "No, you see, I meant that it would be too difficult because I do not have those records. I believe all of her records went with her when she gave this hotel to me." His eyes looked behind Justin and then down at the counter. "I don't believe I can help you."

"You do not have such records here in a storage room?" Justin asked. Justin had agreements with a handful of nice hotels in the city. They would send their patrons to his gaming hell and he would always recommend their establishments for visiting guests. He knew how hotels were run, knew that most worth their salt kept records of their guests because they wanted repeat customers.

"No, I do not."

Justin had every record ever documented at Rodale's. Granted they'd been open less than ten years, still, one never knew if that information would be needed in the future. There was something in the man's mannerisms that bothered Justin. He'd wager the man was hiding something.

"Thank you for your time," he said, then he turned on his heel and retrieved the women.

Clarissa walked passed him back up to the desk. "Pardon me, Sir," she said. "Are you telling me that you did not keep any of the records of previous guests?"

His lips pinched. "No, that is what I was telling your, friend," he said deliberately, "and now what I am telling you."

"Well, that simply makes no sense at all."

"I believe I am the hotelier, not you, madam," he said. "Now good day to all of you."

The three of them did not speak until they were once again encased in the carriage.

"He was obviously lying," Clarissa said boldly.

"I believe so too," Justin said.

"One way to find out," Ella said.

"And that is?" Justin asked.

"Lady Manchester, his cousin, it was her hotel. If she has the records, she would certainly allow you look at them," Ella said, then she frowned. "I'm afraid she suffers from dementia though, so you'll have to hope to catch her on a good day."

"Perhaps today will be that good day," Justin said. He knocked on the carriage ceiling and they stopped. He stepped out, gave the driver the address Ella rattled off for Lady Manchester's and then they were off again.

"I have met Lady Manchester before," Ella said. "So I suppose I shall be the one to introduce the two of you. I do hope she finds that good enough."

"It will have to be. We need to speak with her," Clarissa said.

Not a quarter of an hour later the three of them waited in Lady Manchester's parlor. Unlike the hotel bearing her name, this room spoke of more immediate wealth. Justin sat in the only wooden, non-upholstered chair in the room while his wife huddled closely next to her friend on the settee. When the door opened, the three of them stood.

The lady walked in without the assistance of anyone and seemed completely capable, but a woman followed closely behind her. Once Lady Manchester sat, the other woman promptly wrapped her lap in a blanket, then went to stand behind the woman's chair.

"It's so rare that I get visitors these days," Lady Manchester said.

"Lady Manchester, I'm not certain if you remember me, I'm Ella Atkins. I believe you know my mother, Lady Weaver. These are two of my friends, Mr. and Mrs. Justin Rodale. They'd like to ask you a few questions."

The woman nodded, then looked up to see her guests. Her breath caught when she looked at Justin. "Gracious, you look just like her," she said.

"Who?"

"Simone," she said, then shook her head. "I cannot remember the girl's full name."

Simone. Was his mother's name Simone?

"We'd like to ask you a few questions about Manchester House," he said.

"Thieving bastard took that property right from under my nose, he did," Lady Manchester said with a frown. The woman behind her put a hand on her ladyship's shoulder.

"Don't pat me to calm me, Sally, I speak the truth." She shooed away the woman's hand.

"Your cousin?" Clarissa asked.

"Yes, nasty little man. I bequeathed the entire hotel to my niece, Charlotte, and her husband, but somehow Winston got it put in his name." She shook her head. "I'll never understand it."

"But you owned it and ran it in the 40s?"

She met his gaze again and nodded. "Yes. I simply cannot get over how much you favor Simone."

"Did you keep records of your guests during that time?"

"Primarily the time when you had all the families from France stay with you during the Season," Clarissa added.

"Of course, I kept impeccable records," Lady Manchester said. "My father always told me that you never put anything of importance in the rubbish."

"Do you have them?" Clarissa asked. "The records?"

"Of course not, they're at the hotel. In the basement, precisely right where I left them. A record of every guest and every room they stayed in as well as every pence they spent. I kept meticulous records."

"When we visited there earlier today, your cousin claimed that you had taken all the records with you," Clarissa said.

"Why would I do a silly thing like that?" She pointed a crooked finger at Clarissa. "That man is nothing but a lying fool. Unless he's put everything in the rubbish, then it should all still be there."

"This Simone you speak of," Justin said. "Did you know her well?"

Lady Manchester smiled warmly. "I did, she was a wonderful girl, so full of life and love."

"Did she find love here?"

"She did, but it was not to be. Her family had already arranged a marriage between her and a wealthy Frenchman. She left here quite heartbroken," Lady Manchester said. A wistfulness filled her expression. "She was so very pretty." She looked up at Justin. "You look like her, you know."

"Thank you, my lady," he said, "for your time and your information."

There was only one thing to do now. He had to break into Manchester House to sneak a peek at those records.

Chapter Fifteen

Justin had intended to invite her to accompany him back to the hotel that night, but had changed his mind. It was one thing for him to break into a building, but to bring along his wife and make her a criminal as well…

"Are you going back to Rodale's?" her voice came from behind him.

He considered lying to her, but he'd never been much of a liar. Part of why he'd hated gambling. "No, I am going to Manchester House," he said. "I need this issue resolved. And I want to take a peek at those records before that man decides to destroy them. If he hasn't already done so."

"I'm going with you," she said.

"Chrissy, there is no need for that. If we get caught, there will be nothing I can do to salvage the rest of your good name."

She frowned. "This is infinitely more important than that." When he didn't immediately agree to her going, she popped her fists on her hips. "Take me or I'll simply follow you there," she said defiantly.

"Why do you care so much about this?" he asked. He asked the question before he thought better of it. He wanted her to say that she cared about him, but he knew he'd never hear those words from her. She'd married him because she hadn't had another option.

"You saved me, helped me, I should like to return the favor."

"That is the only reason?"

"Should there be another?" She looked up at him, her eyes wide, her lips parted, all innocence and loveliness.

He shook his head. "Are you wearing that?"

She looked down at her muted green gown and nodded.

"Come then," he said. He assisted her into their carriage. "You will have to follow closely behind me and be quiet. I'd like to get in and out of there without alerting them to our presence."

"Obviously," she said. When he looked at her with raised brows she shrugged. "Else we would be going during the day. I suspected you intended to sneak in. Are we to pose as guests?"

"Not anything so obvious," he said. "We are slipping inside and down to the basement area. If we are seen—" He shook his head. "I don't want to think about what happens if we're seen." If that happened, he'd be lucky if they weren't arrested.

The ride to Manchester House was relatively quick as the late hour made for mostly empty streets. When they arrived, he helped Clarissa down to the street.

Confusion crossed her features; she looked around them. "Where are we?"

"At the back of Manchester House. We can't very well go in the front door."

She grinned. "No, I don't suppose we can. Makes perfect sense." She motioned for him to go on. "Proceed. I shall follow closely."

And she did. They crept into the alleyway behind the hotel and up to the door at the back. "Okay, stay close," he said. They went up to the door and he tried the handle. "Locked," he said. He hadn't expected anything different, which was why he'd brought supplies for such a thing. He retrieved the tool tools from his pocket and stuck them in the keyhole and finagled them around.

"How did you learn how to do that?" she asked.

He looked over his shoulder at her. "They teach this at Eton."

She rolled her eyes.

There was a clicking noise and then he opened the door. He pocketed the tools and peeked inside the door. The darkened room appeared empty. He motioned for her to follow him inside.

There was no way to light a candle until they were down in the basement area, so they'd have to do their best in the dark here. They stood for a moment allowing their eyes to adjust to the darkness. Justin took a step forward. They appeared to be in a corridor that led to an enormous kitchen on one side and a pantry on the other.

"We need to find stairs that go downward," he whispered.

She nodded. The first floor was large. They found parlors and a library, and eventually wound their way back to the lobby they were in the other day.

"There have to be stairs," he said.

"We should have asked Lady Manchester," she said.

Justin stepped around the counter where the Lady Manchester's cousin had stood. Behind there he found a door. "Chrissy," he said with a nod.

She came around to meet him. They stepped through the door, which opened into a room that appeared to be a private office. A quick survey of the space showed another door at the far end. Justin opened it and there found a staircase that led downward.

"Finally," Justin said. He grabbed Clarissa's hand and together they descended into the darkness. Once Justin reached solid floor, he reached into his back pocket and retrieved a candle and match. He struck it and the flame hissed to life. He lit the candle and the small area around them illuminated.

It wasn't an overly large space and filled mostly with boxes.

Clarissa stepped around him. "Shall we get started?" She stepped over to one of the boxes and pulled off the lid. Justin came over to meet her. Inside they found several of the books similar to the book kept at the counter upstairs, the ledger book where guests were logged in. She opened the book on top, but it was from 1872.

"There must be one book for each year," he said. "Thank goodness for good record keeping." He moved over to another box and opened it. The first book he came to was 1857. "Getting closer."

Clarissa came over closer to him and opened another box. "1849. This must be the right box." She withdrew the book and set it aside, and retrieved the one beneath. "1848?"

"I think we really need the previous year," he said. His heart sped. This could be it, if Lady Manchester was right and this Simone was his mother, then he could uncover her name in just a moment.

Clarissa handed him the book. He opened it and flipped through the pages. Page after page of names until the words began to blur.

"There, look, Simone Gauteir, that must be her," she said, looking up at him.

He nodded and looked down where her finger pointed to the decidedly feminine penmanship. There was an address listed. "My apologies to Lady Manchester," he said, then he ripped the page from the book.

"Are you ready?" Clarissa asked.

"I want to look through the rest of these boxes," he said. "That man was nervous for some reason, not wanting people down here. And then something Lady Manchester said. I'm fairly certain he's hiding something." Justin moved to other boxes and still found book after book. But there had to be something down here the man didn't want found. Justin had nearly given up when he caught the sight of a piece of parchment hanging out of the corners of a book. He pulled on it, freeing it from its confines.

"It's her will. I'll read through it later, but if what she said was true and she left this hotel to her niece, then Winston upstairs will have some serious explaining to do." He folded the parchment and put it with the other paper. "Now, let's go."

They went out the same way they'd come in only much quicker. By the time they reached the carriage, Clarissa's breath was shorter.

"That was exhilarating," she said, once they were on their way. "What will you do with her will?"

"Probably pass it to my barrister and allow him to handle the situation."

She reached across and put her hand on his. "I'm glad we found it."

He nodded, but said nothing else. In all honesty, he was glad she was here with him, glad she'd been the one to help him uncover his mother's identity. Ever since he began the search for her, he'd always assumed that it would be Clipps who'd be with him when he received something in the mail. This was better.

Had it been Clipps, though, the moment would have been quite different. Somehow, though, Clarissa simply knew this moment was more important than he wanted to admit. And he knew that he wouldn't have wanted anyone else here with him tonight other than her.

. . .

The following evening Clarissa sat in Justin's study going over her ledgers for Ella's family. Mr. Bembridge had made some significant headway for their financial distress.

Things had been strained between them since the night Justin had come to her bed. He still spoke to her congenially, but not about anything of worth. He hadn't spoken again about the information they'd discovered in Manchester House.

She wanted to ask more about what he intended to do, but she was terrified he would shut her out completely. That he would wake up and realize that his desire for her had waned and there was nothing in their marriage he wanted anymore. So she had not said another word about it. She feared that in bringing him that information, in an effort to become closer to him, she'd pushed him further away.

It was one thing to acknowledge the fact that her husband would never love her. She was trying to come to terms with that. But this indifferent friendliness would never do. She might not be able to discuss matters regarding his mother with him. If he needed to keep that separate from her for a while, then she could abide that. But she could at the very last find her way back to his bed. When he returned from Rodale's she would discuss that with him. Or perhaps, she'd do as he once told her—a seductress takes action. So perhaps she'd merely be in his bed when he arrived home.

The study door opened and she looked up expecting to see her husband. "Did you forget something?" she asked. Then she realized, it was not Justin standing in the study doorway, but rather George.

She came to her feet. "George? What are you doing here?"

"I wanted to have a talk with you, in private," he said. "Obviously I couldn't do so the other evening at the Potterfield Ball because your husband was right there with you. So I came here instead." He eyed her a moment, then smiled. "After I saw Rodale leave for the night."

She came around the desk, intending to see him back out the door. "I don't believe we have anything to discuss, George." There was no longer a reason for her to be pleasant to him. He'd done the unforgivable to her.

"Oh, but we do, Clarissa, we have much to discuss. I will admit that your attempt at coercing me into marriage angered me at first, but I have forgiven you."

She felt her eyebrows rise. "Oh, you've forgiven me, have you?" That was rich. He courted her for more than a year, then he put his hands on her body, yet had chosen to forgive her. Ella had been right about George all along, and Clarissa could kick herself for not trusting her friend sooner.

"Indeed. That was a very naughty thing you did, Clarissa," he said. He took several steps toward her effectively penning her between himself and the desk behind her.

"It was a mistake, a huge mistake," Clarissa said, more to herself than in an effort to apologize.

"Now that you're married, we can come to an agreement." Again he moved toward her.

She braced her hands on the desk behind her.

"An arrangement that would serve both of our needs." He ran a finger down the side of her arm.

How had she ever thought him handsome? Now as he stood before her, she saw nothing but arrogance and pride and a smile that made promises it never kept. "There will be no arrangement between us, George. You should leave. Now."

"No, now is the perfect time for us. Your husband has gone to Rodale's. He won't be home for hours. We have time. Plenty of time to pick up where we left off. Finish what we started." He grabbed her and pulled her against him. His grip on her arms was tight, uncomfortable.

"Unhand me, George. I am a married woman."

"All the more reason that we can now have that affair. I know you want me, Clarissa. I've seen the desire in your eyes. And the way you kissed me. You are a wanton," George said. "I cannot believe it took me so long to see it."

"I am no such thing. And I most certainly do not want you. Justin will be home any moment," she said. But she knew it was untrue. George had been right. Justin had left for

Rodale's and said he probably wouldn't be back until dawn. She was at the mercy of George and his unwanted advances. She supposed she could scream, but she was new in Justin's household and being caught in the arms of another man... there was no way she could explain her way out of that. She certainly didn't want to make Justin look bad.

He rubbed his hands up and down her arms and leaned in to kiss her neck. She pushed at him, shoved at him, but his strength would not be swayed.

"I'll scream."

He laughed. "Good, I like a woman with fight in her. Makes it more interesting."

Oh God, how had she been so very wrong about this man? Or how had Rebecca?

He released one of her arms and rearranged her so that he held both of her arms in one of his hands. He was so strong. With his free hand he slid up her skirt, running his palm against her stocking-clad leg. Her stomach churned.

"Help!" she yelled. It was worth it to try to get someone to help, but he slammed his mouth down on hers effectively stifling her voice. She tried to bite him, kick him, anything to get him off her, but her efforts were in vain. Clarissa's heart pounded so loud, she heard it reverberating in her ears.

And then he was gone, pulled off her and slammed onto the floor.

"Get the hell off my wife and out of my house before I kill you," Justin said. He stood over George's body. "Don't think I won't."

George pulled himself to his feet, rubbing his jaw. "I was just trying to take what she'd offered. Did she tell you the truth about that night?"

Justin slammed his fist into George's face, then nailed him in the stomach. George doubled-over in pain.

"You should consider boxing, Rodale," George said.

"I'll say it again. Get the hell out of my house," Justin said, his tone even, but deadly.

George wiped blood off his lip, then spit a mouthful onto Justin's imported rug. "You can have her."

• • •

The moment George left the study, Clarissa's tears started. Justin gathered her in his arms.

"It's all right now, love, I'm here." He kissed her forehead, smoothed his hand over her hair. When he'd come in the room and seen George on her, he'd nearly lost his mind. He'd wanted to rip the bastard's head off. "I should have killed him."

She gave him a weak laugh. "That wouldn't have solved anything. I certainly don't need you in prison."

"Let's get you upstairs and cleaned up," he said.

• • •

Clarissa woke with a start. The room was still dark and Justin's heavy sleeping form lay next to her, his breathing even. Her heart pounded. He'd taken her to her room the night before, helped her into her night clothes, then he had crawled into bed with her. He hadn't made love to her, merely rubbed her back gently until she'd fallen asleep. And he had stayed in the bed with her.

Her heart swelled knowing what she must do.

She slid from the bed and stood silently watching him

for a moment. He would not understand, no one would, but still it was something she needed to do. She'd waited too long and now it was time to go.

• • •

Justin stretched, and reached over to pull his wife close to him, but the side she'd slept on was empty. Cold and empty. She'd been gone a while. He sat up. Once he'd pulled on some trousers, he walked through the bathing chamber and then on to his room, but there was no sign of her in either place.

He ignored the choking feeling squeezing at him. Her maid, Mary, hadn't seen her, so she'd evidently dressed on her own. She was not in the dining room and no one in the kitchen had seen her. George Wilbanks had gotten into their house the night before without any of the servants being the wiser, what if he'd come back and taken her?

"Mr. Rodale, sir, I'm afraid your wife has left. She hired a hack early this morning," the butler said.

"Why they hell did you let her go?" But Justin didn't wait for a response. He ran up the stairs and finished getting dressed, before returning and yelling for a carriage. In less than twenty minutes he was on the road to the Kincaid townhome. Clarissa was impetuous and…what if she had decided that marriage to him was simply not enough?

He supposed he shouldn't be surprised. Women in his life didn't tend to stick around for very long. He'd already sent a letter to Simone Gauteir, but had yet to hear anything. His mother had left him a long time ago and nothing could be done about that, but he'd be damned if he'd let his wife leave.

He pounded on the front door of the townhome and was greeted by a smiling Vivian. Any other time he'd have asked why she was answering the door herself, but now was not the time.

"Justin?" she said in surprise.

"Is Clarissa here?"

She frowned. "No. Justin, what's happened?"

"No time." He turned and left and jumped back into the carriage and gave the driver Ella's address. The ride there seemed to take an eternity and he was beginning to think he could have run faster when the carriage rolled to a stop.

Again he knocked on the door. When the butler opened it, he demanded an audience with Lady Ella and the man didn't even blink, merely nodded and invited Justin inside.

Ella was evidently already waiting for him. She smiled when he stepped into the room.

"Where is she?"

"She went to Ashford Hall," Ella answered without reservation. "She stopped by here early this morning, very upset. I made her take one of our carriages so she was with a trusted driver."

He shook his head. She had left him. They hadn't even been married a full month and she had left.

"Everyone she has ever loved has left her," Ella said.

"I beg your pardon?"

"Clarissa. Everyone she's ever loved, they've all died or walked away," Ella said.

"I'm not the one that left."

Ella held up one hand. "Be patient with her, Mr. Rodale. She is frightened."

"If she thinks I'm going to let her go without a fight." He shook his head. "She is my wife."

Ella nodded, then gave him a big smile. "Then go. Go get her."

. . .

Clarissa walked quietly through the gardens of Ashford Hall. She caught sight of the large oak up ahead. Its sprawling limbs arched out and swooped down creating an umbrella to the grounds beneath it. When she'd awakened that morning she'd known precisely what she had to do.

Nearly her entire life she had tried to be someone she simply could not be. Someone she didn't even want to be. She'd never be the perfect lady like Rebecca. Not for lack of trying, but she'd only ended up compromised and married to a most unexpected man.

The grave markers lined up in short rows.

She found the one she sought and knelt to the ground. She was quiet for a moment before she began to speak.

"Oh, Rebecca, I fear you would believe I have made such a mess of things. Though I tried very hard I was unable to marry the man you'd selected for me." She took a deep breath. "But had you seen the truth of George's character, you never would have selected him. He is not a nice man at all. Oh, he certainly knows how to behave as such, when the situation demands it, but underneath all that charm, he is quite horrid." She exhaled slowly. "I know you never cared for Justin, you always thought he was so fussy." Clarissa chuckled. "I think you would feel differently about him now. He's grown into a wonderful man. And heaven's above he is so handsome.

"I expected that simply because George had been born of noble blood that that somehow made him a true gentleman. Consequently, I expected the very opposite of Justin simply because he'd been born out of wedlock." She sighed and smiled. "But Justin Rodale is more of a gentleman than another other man I know. He is so noble and honorable.

"I think you would see how he's changed. I think you would like him, I hope you would. But it wasn't just George you were wrong about, Rebecca, it was me." Clarissa shook her head. "I've tried so hard, all these years, to be a lady like you taught me. To be genteel and proper and polite. But I'm none of those things. I'm smart and I'm good with numbers. After Charles died I fired our solicitor and managed the family money by myself. And I did a good job. I've even continued in the charade and helped a dear friend with her family's financial situation.

I've hid in darkened corners of a museum and allowed a man to steal a kiss. And I enjoyed it, felt exuberant and alive." She found herself smiling now as happiness surged through her. "I broke into a hotel, Rebecca! Oh how scandalized you would have been, but I loved every adventurous moment of it."

She paused a moment, ran her hand over Rebecca's carved name. "I don't know that I'll ever have that love that you and Charles had as I don't know if Justin will ever love me in return. But there is something in Justin's eyes, just as you said there would be when I found the right man. I've seen it. If I'm completely honest with myself it's been there in his eyes the whole time."

How had she missed that? She'd been so consumed with trying to marry George that she'd missed the man standing in front of her. If she wasn't so damned relieved by the way things had worked out, she'd feel an utter fool. Somehow she'd made all the wrong choices, but ended up in the most perfect situation.

"I do wish you were still here, Rebecca to know me as I truly am and to know my husband. But I no longer feel like I need to live my life as you would have wanted me. I no longer feel as if your standards are the only standards. I'd like to hope that you would love me and would accept him, but even if you didn't I'd still choose him."

She was quiet a moment while she stared at the carving of Rebecca's name until the letters blurred. "I believe I love him," she said.

"He loves you too," a voice said from behind her.

Clarissa stood and turned to see Justin standing there with a hand-pulled bunch of pansies in his fist. Tears filled her eyes. "Rebecca loved pansies, they were her favorite."

"I know. I remember you told me that once." He closed the distance between them and placed the flowers on Rebecca's grave.

"How long have you been standing there?"

"Long enough." He took a deep breath. "I came here ready to fight for you, ready to make you come home with me if I had to. I thought you'd left me."

The tears fell, chilling her cheeks. "Never. No matter what, I'd never leave you." She smiled up at him. "You were going to make me come home with you?"

"If I had to."

"I can't believe you thought I'd left."

He shook his head. "I didn't know how you were feeling since last night. Since George—are you certain you don't want me to kill him?"

She laughed. "Of course not. Though you could have hit him a few more times."

"I've banned him from Rodale's. He will no longer be using our gaming hell as his cover," Justin said.

"You did?" She looked up at him, his intense amber eyes, the handsome chiseled jaw. Her husband. "Did you mean what you said?"

"About?"

"Do you truly love me?"

"Yes." He pulled her to him, squeezing her tight. "I love you, Chrissy. Or do you prefer Clarissa?"

"No, I've grown quite fond of Chrissy. But only with you."

"Yes, only with me. Forever only with me."

Epilogue

Clarissa ran up the stairs of Rodale's as quickly as her skirts would allow her. If Justin would simply agree to purchase her some trousers, this would be so much easier. She clutched her reticule to her chest and she reached the top and opened the outer offices.

Clipps looked up from his new desk and smiled. "Morning Mrs. R."

"Morning, Basil. Can't talk, have an important letter for Justin," she said. She breezed through into the larger office, the office she now shared with her husband.

"My love, I told you I would be home by dinner." He grinned sinfully at her. "Couldn't wait to see me?"

She retrieved the envelope from her reticule. "This came in the post." She handed it to him.

He looked down and then back up to her. "It's from Paris."

She nodded. "Read it!"

He opened it and stood there quietly for several

moments. Then he looked up at her. "It's her," he said with a smile.

Clarissa smiled and then threw her arms around her husband. "I knew we'd find her. What does she say?"

"That she would love to come to London and meet me. She has other children. It would seem I have two sisters."

"Oh, Justin, I love you so much," she said. Her heart swelled so much she feared it would burst.

"I couldn't have done this without you. I never would have looked in the right place." He glanced back at the letter. "She seems quite happy I found her."

"I'm certain she is. She'll love you. It's simply impossible not to."

OTHER BOOKS BY ROBYN DEHART

THE FORBIDDEN LOVE SERIES
A Little Bit Wicked

A Little Scandalous

THE MASQUERADING MISTRESSES SERIES
No Ordinary Mistress

For Her Spy Only

Misadventures in Seduction

Undercover with the Earl

About the Author

As a life-long lover of stories and adventure, it was either become a stuntwoman for the movies or live out those adventures from the safety of her PJ's and computer. Award-winning author, Robyn DeHart chose the latter and couldn't be happier for doing so. Known for her unique plotlines and authentic characters, Robyn is a favorite among readers and reviewers. Publishers' Weekly claims her writing to be "comical and sexy" while the Chicago Tribune dubs her "wonderfully entertaining." Robyn is also a four-time RT Bookclub Reviewers' Choice award nominee, and a three-time RomCon Reader's Crown nominee. Look for two new series coming from Robyn in 2013. Robyn lives in Texas with her brainy husband, two precocious little girls, and two spoiled cats. You can find Robyn online at her website or at one of her group blogs, the Jaunty Quills or Peanut Butter on the Keyboard.